THE *Sepia* SEASON

THE *Sepia* SEASON

A Novel

DONNA L. HUISJEN

Published in the United States by Credo House Publishers,
a division of Credo Communications, LLC, Grand Rapids, Michigan
www.credohousepublishers.com

ISBN: 978-1-625860-25-5

Cover and interior design: Sharon VanLoozenoord

Printed in the United States of America

First edition

CONTENTS

"Call it a clan, call it a network, call it a tribe, call it a family. Whatever you call it, whoever you are, you need one."

—JANE HOWARD

"A father to the fatherless, a defender of widows,
is God in his holy dwelling.
God sets the lonely in families."

(PSALM 68:5–6)

MAIN CHARACTERS

Adele (**Nanna** to her grandchildren)
Sixty-three-year-old widow, homeowner and head of household.

Nadine
Adele's sixty-six-year-old autistic sister, who has lived with the family for almost thirty years.

Lauren
Adele's thirty-two-year-old daughter, who following her divorce from Gage nearly three years earlier has lived, along with their three children, with Adele and Nadine.

Grant
A never-married man in his early thirties, employed and taking night classes in the interest of an eventual career change. Enters the story in the third chapter as Lauren's classmate in pre-calculus.

Lannie (**Alanna**)
Lauren and Gage's six-year-old daughter.

Lexie (**Alexa**)
Lauren and Gage's four-year-old daughter.

Luke
Lauren and Gage's two-year-old son.

Gage
Lauren's ex-husband, currently living with Mallory and her three children.

Mallory
A thirties-something, never-married mother of three.

Daisy
Mallory's six-year-old daughter.

Jovanny
Mallory's five-year-old son.

Rory
Mallory's two-year-old son.

January

 Nadine

*"Autism is as much about what is abundant as what is missing,
an over-expression of the very traits that make
our species unique."*—PAUL COLLINS

She sat stone still, or appeared to. Her chiseled features may have distorted the impression, since one foot clearly pivoted up and down in a motion that set the chair to moving slowly, with a creak each time its rockers reached their limit. It wasn't that she appeared preoccupied—more absent, either biding time or unconcerned with its passage. The ticking of the clock added dissonance, for the timing was off—like competing songs, each following its own tempo. The set of Nadine's features looked more penetrating than stern; there was an intense, and conceivably perverse, expression on her face that was as off-putting as the vying rhythms.

Her sister Adele, who from long experience trusted Nadine alone for short periods but was usually particular about being home when six-year-old Lannie breezed in from school, had taken her two younger grandchildren, Lannie's sister and brother, with her on a short, time-sensitive errand. She hoped the two mischief makers, old and young, could be trusted in one another's company for a little while.

The pulse changed abruptly as the little girl (who had made the two-block walk with a neighbor mom and her daughter) threw open the door, calling, "Mail. Boxes!" followed irrelevantly by

"Your hair's all ec-static. It's sticking right up!" Nadine's glittering eyes and slightly accelerated rocking indicated that her interest had been piqued. Lannie shucked her backpack, which dropped to the floor, disgorging a colorful pile of miscellaneous papers in various stages of dilapidation, signified by random creases and furrows, along with what appeared to be a single gym shoe and a number of mismatched mittens and partially consumed eatables. In each hand she grasped an oblong box; a short stack of mail was wedged in the crook of her arm.

With a clucking sound her great-aunt snatched one of the boxes, and the two set about revealing their content. Lannie, first at this, announced "Checks." A quick perusal of the envelopes (Nadine still held the reading advantage) revealed a number of statements, one of which for some reason she saw fit to tear open. "Bill," she chortled in the easy shorthand Lannie had introduced. And it was Nadine, quicker on the draw and on a roll now, who made the connection.

The medical bill, covering the patient portion of Adele's recent cataract surgery, was large, in excess of a thousand. Glancing, Lannie registered only a bigger number than she'd encountered in first-grade math. "Let's pay," Nadine suggested conspiratorially, wrapping her fingers around the pencil and calling out "*Surprise!*" to no one in particular.

Not sure how to proceed, Nadine enhanced her concentration by protruding the tip of her tongue between her rows of teeth, her gaze alternating between the bill with its array of numbers and the blank check with its array of fields. Lannie, having no interest in spectating, wandered off toward the kitchen in quest of a snack. When she returned with cookies—three apiece since the opportunity presented itself—Aunt Nadine dropped the pencil readily enough and dove in, crumbs spraying in her eagerness.

Adele

*"You can complain because roses have thorns, or you
can rejoice because thorns have roses."*—ZIGGY

Her legal name was Adell, which she'd hated since childhood. It was only upon encountering a transformative spelling as a young teen that she'd shortened the second cursive *l* to an *e*, gentling the name into a good fit. A sixty-three-year-old widow, she had taken in her mentally challenged older sister nearly three decades earlier. Forced by this circumstance to leave the workforce in her mid-thirties, she had devoted herself to raising her five children, along with caring for Nadine. Roderick (Roddy) had accepted the added dependent with his characteristic genial spirit. Until his rapid decline eleven years earlier of pancreatic cancer he had functioned as breadwinner and family champion.

At the time of his death only Lauren, the youngest, remained in the house, but the tension caused by her rocky relationship with Gage had led to a break from her childhood home. The young couple had married and indulged their wanderlust for more than five years, after which Lauren's pregnancy with Al-anna (Lannie) had altered their course, force-fitting—or at least forcing—them into the groove of serious responsibility. Alexa (Lexie) had trailed her big sister by only eighteen months, with little Luke, now two, the unexpected icing on a cake that was by that time stale and crumbling.

Gage's unreliability had increased with his drinking, and after his domestic assault on his very pregnant wife, Lauren had filed for divorce and put into place a personal protection order for herself and the children. That accomplished, she had closed the door on the small rental, packed up, and packed in with Adele and Nadine.

Accustomed to a full house and anticipating a reprieve from Nadine's sole companionship, Adele had taken in the family willingly enough; the large older home accommodated all, and Adele was, if anything, more acclimated to childrearing now than she had been her first time around. Lauren found it convenient to spend one evening each week pursuing her associate's degree at the local community college, leaving Adele free to manage the day-to-day household operations.

Nadine was compliant enough. "Always blessed!" was her

stock in trade and invariable answer when questioned about her well-being. Where she'd picked this up no one remembered, but there was truth to it. Her eyes gleamed more than twinkled—an intense, unblinking, 100-watt gleam that neither varied nor burned out, so intense it seemed to blind her like stage lights; there was little evidence of incoming data making it through. When in the company of others—or more accurately in their vicinity—she had a way of barking out a periodic random "Pleased to meet you!" She was clearly happy, and blessed to be so.

Truth be told, Nadine had never to Adele's knowledge properly *met* anyone. Attempting to engage her was a disconcerting experience. Even when she did, upon command, respond to a request to "look me in the eye," her focus seemed slightly off center, enough to increase the arc of disconnect with the intervening distance. One never quite knew where (or if) Nadine was looking—either in terms of which outward direction or whether outward or inside. Nadine had about her a seemingly sophisticated trickiness that threw off the uninitiated.

Lexie

"*Did you have fun this morning, Lexie?*"
"*Yea. I played with Haley.*"
"*That's nice. Is Haley your size?*"
"*No, Nanna. Haley's her size, not my size.*"

Dropping off Lexie at preschool, Adele watched her swish off in her snow pants, backpack thumping, knitted cap slightly crooked and anchored by "ear mugs." Ready to back out, she noticed the child slip and fall on an icy patch of sidewalk and turn a beseeching gaze in Adele's direction, question marks in her eyes: *Do I stand up and continue walking, or cry so Nanna will comfort me?* From the corner of her eye Adele watched the little girl come to a stand, throw one more resigned glance in her nanna's direction, and head off toward the knot of teachers and children.

Miss Tish, one of two teachers, met her with a grin, accompanied by a bear hug that nearly threw her off balance again. Since the weather was bright, the boys and girls were to enjoy ten minutes on the play equipment before the regular routine. Lexie's gaze met her special friend Haley's, and the playmates, relieved of their packs, ran off in the direction of the swings.

But something unexpected stopped them. Over by the part of the chain link fence with the opening for walkers was an unfamiliar presence. A tall, blonde man in a surprisingly thin beige jacket stood, or partially leaned, arms resting on the top of the fence, just ahead of where its slightly extended barbs would have cut him. He was smiling broadly, his gaze directed toward the two little girls.

Though they had not been addressed, Haley took the initiative of warding off any possible confrontation, declaring with some finality, "We're not asposeta talk to strangers." Lexie averted her gaze, from shyness or in embarrassment at Haley's taking so hard a line. The man's smile only broadened, as though to signal an obvious exception to *that* rule. One hand lifted slightly; between two of the ungloved fingers a Jolly Rancher pivoted hypnotically.

No conversation did ensue. There was no time, as Miss Celine, the other teacher, was approaching in full scuttle. Evidently intimidated, the stranger took his cue, disappearing with an enthusiasm that surprised the gaping girls. As the children were herded into the building (the promised playtime had been exceptionally short), Lexie was aware both of an unusual flurry of adult activity and of a slightly charged tenseness in the atmosphere.

Gage

"*Cries for help are frequently inaudible.*"—TOM ROBBINS

Gage had taken up with Mallory after a brief internet acquaintance. She herself had three small children; Daisy and Jovanny were half Hispanic, while little Rory had African American features offset by startling blue eyes. Mallory was at this point heavily pregnant with Gage's fourth child. Reported suspicions of child neglect, based more on the family's history of homelessness than on acts of negligence, had landed her a spot on the Child Protective Services (CPS) radar screen, and both she and Gage were antsy about the risks of her giving birth in West Michigan. Indefinite plans were underway to leave the state in early February when her monthly government stipend had been deposited to her card. The target destination was unspecified; the net was being cast wide, though somewhere south made sense.

Transportation was the bugaboo. Gage had attempted a fast one, texting an acquaintance with a request to meet the family at a used car dealership during the man's lunch hour. The idea had been a long shot, with the cagey salesman all too eager to cooperate. Gage, so the story would go, would need a very temporary cosigner—two weeks max—till his credit had cleared. The timing was strategic, with the family intending to set out in their SUV just before the friend would begin to grow suspicious.

This ruse having failed, the distance between Michigan and somewhere South still seemed insurmountable. A clunker nudged along by a prayer presented the only conceivable option. All kidding aside, Gage acknowledged, he'd tried that prayer thing— had considered himself a believer back with Lauren before they'd taken off on their five-year nomad spree. That had been before the onset of responsibility, which hadn't set well with him at the time. No, he conceded ruefully now, God would probably have no interest in hearing from good ole' Gage. Not now of all times after the fast one he'd just attempted. He could only hope the Lord was moved of his own accord by need. But prayer—an out-and-out request—that would be audacious!

Lannie

"Nanna, on the new Earth will there be January?"
"Nanna, if there's no death in the new Earth,
what will happen when I pick a flower?"

Lannie, tucked in bed by Adele on one of those evenings when Lauren was away at class, was full of questions about the coming new Earth, delighting in all the biblical answers Adele could think of. The two covered the issue in the Bible's figurative language, so accessible to the young, moving from the resurrected bodies of all who had "passed on" in Christ (Lauren insisted on this euphemism with her children, uncomfortable herself with death) to lions sleeping with lambs to babies playing over the holes of poisonous snakes to crowns to streets of gold and even to the "mansions" (the old King James term more typically translated "rooms") Jesus is preparing for us.

Adele looked forward to her reunion with Roddy—whatever that relationship was to look like—and to a forever life devoted to worship but also alive with culture and reading and classes and pets and gardening and hobbies and the arts and travel and scenic beauty; this time-locked initial phase of eternity, she knew, was a blip in comparison to what lay ahead. Still she chose to indulge her granddaughter's bent toward the fanciful and dreamy. After all, God had chosen to reveal "precious" little of the detail of this future and final phase of eternity, only whetting the human appetite on a need-to-know basis. Captivated with her version, Lannie informed Adele as she nestled in to her comforter that she couldn't wait to dream about the new Earth.

Lauren

"You don't have to say everything to be a light.
Sometimes a fire built on a hill will bring interested
people to your campfire."—SHANNON L. ALDER

Her intentions had been of the best. An outing with fashion-savvy little girls, though, was different altogether from a morning spent with an opinionated, antsy, and tightly restrained two-year-old boy. Confinement in a shopping cart was doing nothing to improve the tot's mood, though it was serving to distract his mom from his unending demands. It wasn't often Lauren found an opportunity for unrestricted window-shopping. Given her nearly empty wallet the danger of overspending was nil, but Luke would have preferred ten minutes exploring the mall's recessed jungle gym to more than an hour watching his mom sniff cologne samples and finger negligees.

At last, unable any longer to restrain her son, Lauren wheeled the cart to the department store exit, lifted out the now kicking toddler, and struggled with her flailing bundle into the blinding sunlight.

Seated at last behind the wheel, her raging child's activity once again restricted by a seatbelt whose grip he couldn't dislodge, she heaved a sigh before starting the car and pulling out. Not ready to cut short her altered routine, she turned in the direction of a nearby McDonalds with Playplace. Two $.49 soft vanilla cones wouldn't break the bank, and Luker could release his pent-up energy on the toys before their return home.

Minutes later mother and son, his outlook much improved, were engaging their cones—Luke's method alternated between plunging his face into the ice cream and tentatively touching it with the wriggling tip of his tongue. In an attempt to slow the relentless drip cycle, Lauren swirled his ice cream around her tongue several times, handing the soggy cone back to her son to gnaw until his interest waned. Minutes later, swiping at his shirt half-heartedly with a pile of napkins, she scooped him from the high chair, removed his boots, and deposited him in front of the stairs to the play equipment.

Luke's squeals signified his delight, and his high-pitched voice assured her that her sociable boy was engaged in an avid two-year-old conversation. His being out of sight but not earshot, Lauren relaxed over the leftovers of both cones. Moments later two heads of nearly identical height bobbed into view at the bottom of the covered slide. As the boys emerged from around the corner, Lauren smiled at the contrast: her towhead grasped the hand of an olive-skinned boy, his profuse black curls in contrast to Luke's pin-straight strands. Two sets of cerulean blue eyes on otherwise very different faces twinkled in synch.

A heavily pregnant mom with flushed face and straggly

blonde hair beginning to betray darker roots—the picture of exhaustion—caught Lauren's glance with a smile so wry that for a second it seemed beseeching. Lauren—sated now with ice cream and little boys—flashed her best "I've been there!" smile, and two moms exchanged a gaze of empathic fellow feeling.

Daisy

"Real strength is neither male nor female; but is,
quite simply, one of the finest characteristics that any
human being can possess."—MISTER ROGERS

Miss Vanessa, a somewhat older miss than the little girl had previously encountered but one she associated with what a grandma must be like, smiled at Daisy's approach. The volunteer, seated at the low table immediately outside this first-grade classroom, feet separated and slightly turned inward but knees touching in a triangle pattern, listened each morning as one child after another stumbled or breezed through their last night's book.

The "Book in a Bag" program was both economical—the photocopied black-and-white books had been collated and stapled by the teachers during a summer several years earlier—and efficient. Many had since that time been colorized by spills or the scribbles of younger brothers or sisters. By this point in January the children ranged in ability level from "B," Daisy's designation, to "J," already attained by the class prodigy, Felix, despite his single mother's inability with English.

Many of the little ones were coached by parent, grandparent, or older sibling every night in preparation, but Mallory's preoccupation with survival issues precluded such attention to detail. Daisy's own occupation with these issues was exerting a double whammy; with her mind previously engaged, the words on the page remained a shame-inducing puzzle. Daisy was one of many in this situation, causing the harried social worker down the hall to deal with an overload. The routine in the hallway was punctuated many mornings by children in the throes of a meltdown being walked or dragged in the direction of Miss Torne's office, an aide on one side firmly grasping them under one arm with the slight but durable principal, Mrs. Graham, taking the other.

Hallway activity abounded, with classes being escorted at regular intervals to music, art, gym, media, library, lunch, recess, skill-targeted reading or math groups, or testing of one kind or another. The lunch lady wielding her flatbed "truck," picking up the leftover breakfast paraphernalia sitting outside each door and substituting tubs of morning veggie snacks, attempted with apologies to make her way between tables with their scattered aides and volunteers. Children running errands, perhaps escorting a sick classmate to the office or toting the class's returned books to the library with a fellow "friend," the school's designation for each student, met the custodian emptying the trash and recycle bins also deposited outside the doors. Once each morning a city police officer made his rounds, strolling in studied leisure through the seeming confusion, taking note of business as usual. The children were fortunate to be enrolled in a well-administered school catering to an at-risk population; the hubbub camouflaged purposeful activity with surprisingly few glitches.

On this Thursday morning Daisy, who had missed the past three days (she was nearly always absent on Mondays, a byproduct of Gage's weekend binging), appeared truly ill. The dark eyes encircled by puffy skin were dulled by flu and disengaged from the half-smile that seemed forced from a different face. Noncommittally turning the first page, the little girl sighed with a slight quiver of her lip, announcing bravely to Vanessa, "Ill try not to cry . . . or hurt!"

Arabelle

"You can't keep a good man down—or an over affectionate dog."—ANONYMOUS

Adele pushed back far enough in the recliner for the footrest to pop into position. Lexie, on her lap, book opened to the first page, leaned against Nanna's chest in anticipation, a thumb pushing its way slightly into her mouth before, in autonomic memory, removing itself, the fingers and wet thump splaying companionably instead across Adele's forearm. Arabelle, Lauren's fast-growing lab-mix pup, seeing her opportunity to share the goodwill, bounded up, settling atop the open book after a few profuse licks of Adele's cheeks and a partial turnaround in quest of optimal positioning.

"Get down, Arabelle. My lap's all full," Adele chided with a nudge to the carpet. *"Sit!"*

Lexie, jumping to a standing position on one of Adele's legs, called out, "Stand up for Jesus, Arabelle!" The tail wagging increased in velocity.

"You're very silly" (to Lexie).

Flattered: "Thank you!"

Mallory

"Childhood, after all, is the first precious coin that poverty steals from a child."—ANTHONY HOROWITZ

The opening month of 2014 was boding a winter to remember—or preferably to forget—in West Michigan. The repeated phenomenon of a polar vortex (a term no one seemed to remember from previous years) was resulting in one of those "once-in-a-century" weather events, relentlessly hammering the city with snowstorm upon blizzard. At least Mallory hoped so (the once-in-a-century thing, that is), although the as yet poorly fleshed out prospect of "south"—becoming more urgent as her belly and ankles swelled in synch—brought with it an equally imprecise dream of luxuriating through balmy winters.

Having been evicted from an inner-city efficiency due to the rent being in arrears, followed by voluntarily quitting the downtown shelter—where men were housed separately from women and children, and doors were closed to all during the daytime hours—the family, including Gage, had taken up residence in a single bedroom with two queen-sized beds and a kitchenette in a lower-end suburban hotel. The weekly rate offered the carrot of a discount, but Gage and Mallory still found the price exorbitant—much more than that of a small apartment, should their credit score have made that an option.

No matter where they ended up, especially during the cold months, cabin fever was a given; the prospect of a snow day, so tantalizing to most children, tended to throw Jovanny, Mallory's kindergartner, into a funk. On this particular morning the overnight snowfall made the parking lot impassable. The resident snowplow driver with his valiant little truck—old and lacking in horsepower—was struggling to make inroads. But the vehicle had a tendency to break down partway through the job; also, in compensation for its limited oomph the driver had to gun it with every pass, frightening Mallory at the thought that one of her older children, waiting for the bus, might be scooped up or shoved along with the snow.

Jovanny, stir crazy from lack of stimulation and running space, awoke with an eye toward the ribbon of school closing information running across the bottom of the television screen. Unable to read, he had come to recognize the letters denoting his district. Mallory, who had already gotten news of the school system's closure, informed him of the inevitable. But Jovanny was insistent: "No, I want to see if *summer* is closed" (he meant cancelled, she recognized). For all Mallory knew, given the inauspicious start to the year, it just might end up that way!

Rory

*"There is no trust more sacred than the one the world holds
with children. There is no duty more important than ensuring
that their rights are respected, that their welfare is
protected, that their lives are free from fear and want
and that they can grow up in peace."*—KOFI ANNAN

While Mallory's Bridge Card (equivalent to the old "food stamps") was invaluable for groceries (not that it was easy to provide suitable microwavable meals, prepared in stages for five), it fell short when it came to incidentals like cosmetics and toiletries. Mallory had recently taken to her knees, despite her bulging belly, hand-scrubbing the ever-proliferating piles of laundry in the bathtub with a bar of hand soap.

Just yesterday Gage, frightened at the prospect of the uncertain transplantation down South, had grabbed at a straw in an attempt to assure himself he was taking a proactive stance. Rory, at two, he advised Mallory in a matter-of-fact tone, no longer needed disposable diapers. And with a new one on the way . . . He recalled clearly that his own Lannie had virtually trained herself at around that age and that Lauren had been working with Lexie on this life skill at the time of the couple's separation. While Mallory, alarmed, explained that Jovanny as a boy had required considerably more time for this transition, Gage was insistent. Even if nothing else was going their way, this had to work!

At this moment little Rory, spread eagle, was seated precariously at the extreme front end of the oval; it required all his arm strength to support his perch and balance above the cavern. For some unaccountable reason Mama was insisting that his pee-pee point downward and was holding it in that position. The soiled bed sheet was rolled in a ball next to the front door after last night's accident, which had raised loud protests from Rory's bedmates on both sides. The scrubbed mattress was airing in the hope it would dry by naptime.

To the overtaxed mother it seemed as though her own bodily fluid had sprung a lethal leak; head throbbing, she envisioned her water breaking, repeatedly and continually, without producing the long-for relief of the onset of labor and the prospect of a finale.

Rory's expressive blue eyes were puddled question marks. Was this some bizarre new form of punishment? At last, unable to bear the suspense, he dared broach the question: "Are you happy at me?"

Luke

*"A wise parent humors the desire for independent
action, so as to become the friend and advisor when his
absolute rule shall cease."*—ELIZABETH GASKELL

Being alone with Nanna and Aunt Nadine during the mornings had its benefits, but Luke missed his sisters, Lexie in particular, and longed in an unformed and only mildly informed way for his own "skoo" days. Having visited preschool with Nanna on two or three impressive occasions during the first semester, he entertained visions of a regular fare of decorated cupcakes with colorful napkins, cups of lemonade, and cookies, along with racks of picture books, shelves stacked with toys, rhythm instruments, and CDs. Some initiation in the church nursery—a pleasant hour for those old enough to have overcome their separation anxiety—had convinced him of the positives of skoo. Why he too couldn't attend was a question beyond his processing ability.

Luker decided one Saturday morning that the time had come. No one was currently in the living room, so he negotiated his own hat, boots, and coat (mittens attached)—only the zipper eluded him. Luke was prepared for his foray into the world, lacking only a backpack. This he solved with the addition to his getup of Nanna's long-handled knitting bag, sans the skeins, needles, and partially finished slippers, which he left on the floor. The handle over his neck would have choked him had the bag been heavy; as it was it only trailed behind him like an ill-fitting cape.

Opening the big door with Arabelle, a'quiver with anticipation, at his side, he slipped through in synch with her, she nearly tripping him with her already muscled lunge. Arabelle's presence proved a godsend: her sharp and exuberant barking, along with the flapping front door and telltale pile of knitting paraphernalia, alerted the household. The lab, who had never ventured outside leashless before, encircled Luke on the front walk in an ecstasy of abandonment, finally toppling him just as Lauren and Adele burst through the door.

Jovanny

Life has a way of taking you past your wants and hopes. Instead, it drops you in front of what you need." —SHANNON I. ALDER

Jovanny, Mr. Cruz noticed, resisted gym. The other kindergartners equated the running, jumping, throwing, scuttling, and game playing with an organized extension of recess, but this little boy, engaging enough otherwise and apparently healthy, shied away from physical activity. Based on an impromptu meeting in the hall with Miss Gentry (his teacher) and Mrs. Graham (the principal), an agreement was reached that intervention was called for. Mrs. Graham reached the hotel front desk, leaving a message requesting an initial visit with his mom.

Before this could take place Miss Gentry accidently resolved the issue. Asking the children to remove their shoes for a floor activity, she couldn't help but notice Jovanny's uncharacteristic enthusiasm, as well as his quick, agile, and coordinated movement. Was there something about Mr. Cruz, or the size or nature of the gym, that intimidated him? The answer came when, glancing at the shoes strewn alongside the activity rug, her eye caught the small size of one worn pair. She paused for a moment before the *aha!* hit her. Twenty minutes later a beaming Jovanny, fitted with an almost new pair of size twos from last year's lost and found, discovered the joys of unrestricted movement.

Adele's Devotion: A January Reading

EVERY INTRICACY

**"Out of the north he comes in golden splendor;
God comes in awesome majesty."** (JOB 37:22)

Scottish poet William Sharp captures for me much of winter's tranquil beauty in the following snapshot: "There is

nothing in the world more beautiful than the forest clothed to its very hollows in snow. It is the still ecstasy of nature, wherein every spray, every blade of grass, every spire of reed, every intricacy of twig, is clad with radiance."

Winter specializes in close-ups. From beads of water dangling uniformly from berries to the "tinkling" wonder of ice-encased branches to the steady drip of sun-touched icicles to filigreed snowflakes to telltale tracks across an otherwise mirror-smooth snow pack, winter's detailed wonders favor contemplation. And yet its unbroken vistas can soothe and satisfy the most farsighted soul. If you're by nature a winter appreciator, enjoy the season. If you're eager for spring, it isn't too late to retrain your eyes and heart to respond to January's own brand of golden splendor and awesome majesty.

February

Gage

"Never take a person's dignity: it is worth everything
to them, and nothing to you." —FRANK X. BARRON

To the surprise even of himself, Gage had come into possession of a high-mileage older station wagon that announced its own "rust belt" origins, and on the strength of determination and unacknowledged providence the family found its way to the Smokies of North Carolina. Out of funds and vehicular reliability but falling in love with the scenery, they endured a couple of near-freezing nights parked at a rest stop (Where were the sundrenched days and balmy nights Mallory had envisioned?). The wagon, a two-seater, allowed the two boys to stretch out in the area behind the second seat, while Daisy claimed for the first time ever her very own "room"—in the sense of space—on that middle seat. Gage ran the heater intermittently, and the restroom facilities and lobby area, open 24/7, afforded periodic full-body warmth.

Gage devoted the days to exploring the real estate situation, not that he was in a chooser position. To his gratification the small town—enjoying its winter hiatus from tourism—yielded a sprawling and rundown furnished rental to sublet for the off-season, complete with everything but a furnace. It wasn't as though this amenity was out of working order; it simply didn't exist and evidently never had. A single space heater afforded what comfort could be had for sleeping; despite a number of bedrooms to choose from, upstairs and down, Daisy no longer enjoyed her own space but snuggled in a heavily blanketed clot with four other humans!

Sober for a while now (he'd found it necessary after all to replace Jack Daniels with diapers as a need-to-have), Gage's reliability had seen a spike, to Mallory's immeasurable relief. His initial foray into the North Carolina working world yielded a position that involved parking himself alongside the main highway in a chicken costume, waving and beckoning passers-by toward a diner. A more promising opportunity presenting itself, he spent more than sixty hours attempting to cold-sell a vacuum cleaner door to door, remuneration contingent upon his making a designated number of presentations within the week. Having trudged for hours through a relentless icy rain, he ended up not only physically sick and assaulted by a severe bout of depression but penny wiser—though by no means richer.

Lauren

"Our hearts of stone become hearts of flesh when we learn where the outcast weeps." —BRENNAN MANNING

Tuesday evening's commute from the hotel to the downtown campus was always dicey. Despite reports of "black" (unseen) ice and some undeniably slick intersections, Lauren found herself working up her usual slow fume as the driver ahead of her overcompensated for conditions by inching along, brake lights flickering like a July firefly, despite the multiple car lengths he had established between himself and the next car ahead—*way* ahead now.

Why was it, Lauren seethed, thumping her fist on the wheel a few times as a pressure release before running the back of her hand across her forehead, that she *always* encountered these incompetents on Tuesdays? Having to contend with rush-hour traffic, busses, jaywalkers, and a half-block line waiting to enter the community college parking ramp pretty much ensured a head-ache. Her mind's acknowledgment that dinner would wait for a three-hour class had done nothing to convince her stomach. What she needed was a 5-hour Energy Boost, which she didn't have on hand. Her Sierra Mist would have to suffice.

She was cranking the radio in response to the adrenalin spike when the scenario began to unfold. Approaching the intersection on her right (final right turn before the ramp) was an impediment she knew would be trouble. Obviously homeless, and most likely three sheets to the wind, the scruffy, red-faced old gent supported by the overloaded shopping cart was shuffling along in dream-worthy slow motion—though still making better progress than Lauren, now at a standstill. It didn't take long to calculate their respective rates of progress, or to recognize that his unwelcome presence in the crosswalk would equate to another missed light. Why couldn't these people lie low during rush hour?

The indigent had nearly reached the corner, though, when he sagged like a spent bug to the pavement. It took a moment for Lauren's cognition to catch up with her reflexive *"Oh Lord!"* Even after it dawned on her that he'd flopped on the sidewalk heating grate—his destination—she wasn't sure whether she'd mouthed the words as an expletive or a register of shock (they were not a prayer, though they should have been). Moments later, in queue for the shorter than expected line to enter the heated garage, Lauren recognized not only that she was slightly earlier than usual but that her anticipated evening wasn't going to be all that intolerable.

Rory

*"It is an anxious, sometimes a dangerous thing to be a doll.
Dolls cannot choose; they can only be chosen; they cannot
'do'; they can only be done by."* —RUMER GODDEN

The yard held intrigue for the boys, in particular Rory after his months of captivity within four walls, followed much more recently by prolonged confinement in a car seat. Daisy, ordinarily the babysitter by default, preferred to stick like a burr to Mama. This forced Jovanny into the responsibility role, which he handled admirably on behalf of his little brother.

Sticks, stones, berries, dirt, pinecones, acorns, pine needles, thatch, an abandoned nest, and piles of dirtying snow in the shadows—all captivated two little boys on the joint prowl for adventure. Mountain sights and scents were new and invigorating, and the yard, really more a run-up to a sprawling hillside, held an allure wider encompassing than the little boys could take in.

In light of the possibilities, it was an unexpected enticement that ultimately captured Rory's imagination. Somewhere in the litter, beneath a pile of enthusiastically kicked leaves, he found his treasure. Gray with age and exposure, the doll had lain there, waiting, for who knew how many seasons of falling precipitation and leaves? Rory's attention was secured by the doll's obvious disability, four missing appendages. For the duration of the family's stay, this new companion would accompany Rory and Jovanny on their adventures, a silent third party whose presence and "participation" were unquestioningly accepted. Rory would sleep and explore with his newfound friend until unintentionally leaving "Him" (its name) behind on the morning of the family's hurried leave-taking.

Lannie

"Once we believe in ourselves, we can risk curiosity,
wonder, spontaneous delight, or any experience that
reveals the human spirit." —E.E. CUMMINGS

When a challenge exceeded Lannie's six-year-old capability, rather than second-guessing herself this confident oldest child was content to wait for her abilities to catch up with the demands. "Practice makes perfect!" she would quote airily, assuming that the cartwheel would invariably come together with repeated trying. Or "You know what I'm gonna do if there's not a job in the

Olympics for me? I'm gonna be an artist." (*It's always good*, Adele conceded with a chuckle, *to have a backup plan*).

Adele's thoughts carried her back to the previous Wednesday evening—it was amazing how much interaction took place en route to somewhere or other!—when she'd been driving Lannie and Lexie home from a church kids' activity. "How cold is freezing?" Lannie had inquired from the back seat. Having been raised pre-Celsius, Adele had launched into an explanation of the Fahrenheit and Centigrade scales, adding the less than helpful detail that "we have a zero too, but our zero is thirty-two degrees colder than their zero." Following a momentary pause, the aspiring first-grader had responded thoughtfully, "I prefer the Second-grade scale."

Nadine

"[A]utism is more like retina patterns than measles."
—NAOKI HIGASHIDA

"Hidenseek!" demanded Luke with an exuberance that caught Nadine's attention to the point of eliciting a single sharp clap. "Count!" he called out, demonstrating, "One . . . ," to which she clapped again. Exasperated, "No, one, two, three . . ." Unable based on lack of knowledge to proceed further, he hoped his great-aunt would catch the drift. She appeared to, at least to the extent that the counting continued from her side. Her eyes, though unclosed, didn't seem to follow his progress.

Luke scuttled off to the kitchen where Nanna, her back to him, was working at the sink. Beseeching her with a glance to move over slightly, he opened the cupboard door beneath her and sidled at a crouch into the perfect hiding place, his favorite. Aunt Nadine, tired of counting, had quieted, and Luke was all a'jiggle in anticipation of her advance in his direction. This failing—her gaze had drifted back to the infomercial on the screen—he found it necessary to move the game along through another ploy.

"Here I am!" the little boy squealed in delight, jumping

from his perfect spot and running full tilt toward his great-aunt's rocker. His relief at breaking the suspense was almost palpable. Luke stopped short of dive-bombing her lap—Aunt Nadine's responses were never quite predictable—but launched into a victory jig at her feet. "Here I am!" and, in case that wasn't getting through, "I'm here!"

Nadine, excited now, joined the chorus, shrieking "Here I am" while waving her arms in the air from side to side, a motion her tantalized great-nephew was only too happy to mimic. Adele, pleased by their engagement, entered from the kitchen, a cup of steeping Earl Grey clinking in her hands on a saucer. Setting it carefully on the side table, she pushed it back slightly to eliminate the possibility of a direct hit. Nadine, perhaps appreciative in her way, turned toward Adele, her gaze fever-bright. With unexpected speed and velocity she flicked the fingers of both hands only inches from her sister's eyes, crooning, *"Here I am!"*

Lexie

*"There are many fine things which we cannot say
if we have to shout."* —HENRY DAVID THOREAU

Adele and Lexie were on their way home from preschool when they experienced an unwelcome encounter with another vehicle. Adele realized before passing the side street that the too-fast-approaching older-model car wouldn't manage to stop on the sheer ice in the approach to the main road. The teenaged driver was profusely apologetic. It was a good learning experience, Adele assured him, on the unexpected aspects of winter driving. Adele had managed to pull into a driveway, where she and Lexie stood shivering until a preschool mom with a daughter in Lexie's class happened by and offered the little girl shelter in her van before bringing them both home. Lexie was absolutely quiet, both waiting in the van, as reported by her friend's mom, for the police investigation and the tow truck (the damage to Adele's car included a bent front wheel) and immediately after returning home. Adele held off a day before broaching the question of whether the little girl had felt afraid or upset. Lexie's answer was winsome: "No, just kind of serious."

A day or so later Lexie ventured, "Is the TV too loud for you, Nanna?"

"No, it's fine with me."

"It's too loud for me. I'm not the loudest girl."

Adele couldn't help but smile at this flash of self-perception; Lexie at four was beginning to discover some nuances of who she was. Reserved people, Adele knew, tend to recede into the background in a world that values the assertive, the vocal, the outspoken. But how many of those quiet ones who choose their words carefully don't have plenty to say that's worth the listening?

Daisy

"Home is a notion that only . . . the uprooted comprehend." —WALLACE STEGNER

The rambling house and its possibilities held appeal for Daisy, the would-be homemaker. Given Mallory's incapacitation, when she did periodically leave Mama's side it was to make brief forays through the heatless, modestly furnished house, her mind in planning mode. When she could handle rearranging furniture she did so, carefully considering functionality and comfort for her family.

Aware that a baby was soon to be joining them—the cause both of Mama's suffering and of her anticipation—she made arrangement for that too: a folded blanket on the floor near the bed she had chosen for herself and Mama, who would need her assistance. Having no further idea of the demands of a baby (she did wonder about the fit of Rory's diapers in light of the expected smaller size of the new one), she left off further preparation in that area.

Jovanny and Rory would in one sense enjoy separate rooms, but the boys were accustomed to sleeping in a tumbled heap— with her squashed in between. Rory, she reasoned, might become lonely—or cold or scared—in the night and seek comfort along-side his big brother. Gage could bunk wherever he saw fit. Daisy held on to recollections of the darker days of his unpredictabil-ity. Cautious by nature, she held herself in reserve while deliber-ately reserving judgment. Everybody deserved a chance—both Mama and Mrs. Trumball, Daisy's teacher, had said so at differ-ent times—and she would give Gage the benefit of the doubt. Still, her penetrating dark eyes never failed to take in the signs—which she had to admit had been more positive of late.

Adele

"No matter how fast light travels, it finds the darkness has always got there first, and is waiting for it." —TERRY PRATCHETT

Making her way home on a Saturday evening following a choral concert attended with a church friend, Adele, passing the park, found herself mesmerized by what appeared to be a field of diamonds on a blanket of white. In a philosophical frame of mind, she allowed her thoughts to wander to the source of that twinkling, which wasn't wholly intrinsic to the snow. In contrast to the unblinking star shine, it was the reflected light from her car's headlamps that temporarily turned on the switch to that ground-level display.

To what degree, she wondered tangentially as the light re-ceded following her passage, could darkness define a life? And what quality could life hold for someone like that? Life was surely prized by most human beings—by many to the point of a tena-cious struggle for survival. But what could be the impetus for that struggle in the absence of hope? Adele's reflection was mov-ing beyond the bounds of experience; as far back as she could remember her hope had been intact. It was hard to grasp the concept that a *majority* of those peopling the planet might be making their way without a failsafe, groping in a darkness they could only *wish* were penetrable.

Adele had to concede that her life, overall, was good. Yet her circumstances at least some of the time were difficult. How would she feel right now in her identical situation if she didn't live in the light? The reality startled her: this sounded like an impossible scenario.

These partially articulated thoughts ran through her mind in less than a minute—the time it took to pass the park and the block beyond it, pull into her driveway, and click the garage door opener, flooding the scene with artificial light. Stepping as lightly as possible into the quiet house moments later, she paused to give thanks for light, for warmth, for music.

Mallory

"I see enormous loves growing immense and finally crushing me." —ANAÏS NIN

Despite the inauspicious circumstances (Mallory laboring in the tub while the children huddled, bewildered and subdued, in the next room, the coveted space heater in the open doorway halfheartedly wafting luke-warmth into both rooms), the birth was quick and uneventful. Gage rose to the occasion, rising afterward with his third daughter cradled in a bath towel in his arms. The proud father flashed his engaging smile at his girlfriend's other three children before introducing them to their new sister, this one, like both parents, a blonde. The baby's debut was to be her only live sighting; by morning the perfectly formed body was stiff and cold, the face frozen into an expression that could only be described as cherubic.

The benumbed parents dressed her lovingly in the layette they had purchased in Michigan as a symbol of hope, before ushering the children into the dirt backyard (only intermittent piles of blackened snow dotted the landscape) for the burial and "service." Daisy and Jovanny, mouths tightly closed but eyes widened in dismay, declined with vehement head shaking to contribute a few words. Following a recitation of Psalm 23, which Gage knew from his church years with Lauren while she still lived at home and Mallory had memorized somewhere along the way, each of the five

(Rory assisted by Gage) sifted a handful of dirt over the cardboard box. The little boy, silent to that point, protested in little more than a whisper "Her can't breathe!" Life as he'd come to construe it during his two plus years no longer made sense.

Gage remained outside shoveling dirt into the hole and mourning in his own way. Wrapped in a blanket with Rory on the floor, Mallory emitted a moan. Clutching her littlest more tightly, she offered Rory the breast.

Luke

"Surgeons must be very careful
When they take the knife!
Underneath their fine incisions
Stirs the Culprit—Life!" —EMILY DICKINSON

"Who made you?" Adele asked her grandson—a provocative question intended as an intro to a snippet of conversation. Luke's response was immediate and assured; he'd evidently thought this one through: "A docker." While the unexpected reply took his nanna slightly aback, she had to concede that, at least in part, he had this right: Great Physician, Creator, Sustainer, Lover, and . . . at some point in accordance with his perfect plan . . . Taker.

Jovanny

"Children's talent to endure stems from their
ignorance of alternatives." —MAYA ANGELOU

It isn't often, adults assume, that existential questions occupy a child mind. Nothing could be further from the truth. Young minds, though uninformed, beg to be filled and struggle incessantly to expand; new brain synapses are being established at a frenzied rate that would exhaust the settled adult mentality. Is it any wonder little ones—whose growing minds and bodies alike run on full throttle during waking hours—require so much sleep and engage it with such intensity? Five-year-old Jovanny was no exception.

Life and death. How and why. Especially *why?*—a question for which he had not been provided information to establish a believable answer. Such were the issues that played themselves out in Jovanny's mind while Mama lay under the blanket, devastated, with Rory; while Gage refilled the hole with dirt and railed against God and himself; while Daisy huddled, spent, in the corner, willing her mind *not* to entertain those very thoughts. Contrary to assumption, making sense of these questions, and others like them, constitutes a fundamental task of childhood, to be revisited incrementally as maturation allows for better formulated answers—the same answers that will one day underlie a comprehensive worldview.

Adele's Devotion: A February Reading

THE STRETCH

"We also glory in our sufferings, because we know that suffering produces perseverance; perseverance, character; and character, hope." (ROMANS 5:3-4)

These two short verses remind me of February. "Come again!?" you may say. It might be a stretch to equate February with suffering, but if you've grown weary of gradations of gray you'll relate to the association. Biding our time in the bleak midwinter bolsters our patience and toughens our resolve—or at least our resignation. Tolerating winter produces perseverance.

What about character? Well, in the words of Gail Barison, "From winter we learn silence and acceptance and the stillness thickens." Moving right along to hope is a no-brainer. If any single season is conducive to anticipation, it's the approach to spring—far away as this transition might seem more than a month before its official debut, which tends to run ahead in parts of the Midwest of its climatic presentation. More significantly, we're within sight of Lent and its glorious culmination on Resurrection Sunday. If it seems a stretch to flex your enthusiasm right now, just rely on your newly-enhanced character to produce the requisite hope. It won't be all that long now.

March

Gage

"The rhythm of life is intricate but orderly,
tenacious but fragile. To keep that in mind is to build
the key to survival." —SHIRLEY HUFSTEDLER

As though pointed instinctively true north, the family, leaving behind only the slightest mound of memory in the Appalachian dirt—a swelling reminiscent of a first-trimester baby bump—abandoned the rambling house of sorrows and returned to the road, destination West Michigan, this time via Greyhound.

Mallory, languishing in illness, pain, post-partum depression, exhaustion, and shock, found the closest possible imitation of a fetal position and checked out for most of the trip, while Gage—with Daisy's help—entertained the boys. Having lost yet a third beautiful daughter, his thoughts pushed despite his better judgment beyond the boundary of the no-fly zone imposed so inhumanely by court order.

Gage had strayed beyond the limit already in January. Knowing that his oldest, the morally precocious Lannie, would have blown the whistle, he had avoided Parkside, settling for Arborwoods Preschool, where he'd been reasonably certain his second daughter would have followed in her sister's princess slippers. His hunch had paid off first thing on the first sun-swept morning; he had come within only feet of the ever timid Lexie, who, though with no glint of recognition after more than two long years—half a lifetime for her—had kept her head mostly bowed in stranger chagrin.

Gage had meant no harm, despite the Jolly Rancher unaccountably pivoting between two fingers. He'd only wanted the briefest of conversations, but, impressed by the resulting degree of alarm—repeated warnings throughout the week on the local news, thankfully unnoticed by Mallory—had shrunk back from this pursuit, surprised almost to the point of amusement at the notion of himself in the criminal element.

Luke

"God is love. He didn't need us. But he wanted us.
And that is the most amazing thing." —RICK WARREN

Luke at two was puzzled by a question occasionally emerging from the lips of friendly adults: "How are you?" The answer to the query as he heard it ("*Who* are you?") seemed obvious, and his response to still another baffling grownup was understandably tentative: "I'm Luke. I'm a boy."

Simple questions? (Adele had a frustrating tendency to mull things over.) *Perhaps.* But if she stopped to consider the ramifications, she might have to pause longer than Luke did. *How and who are you?* she addressed herself. These queries might have to be turned around to do them justice. It was easy to get them confused—even fused—in her head. To what extent, after all, did *how* she was depend in her mind on *who* she was . . . or viewed herself to be? *Oh bother!* If little ones thought half this much (and she suspected they did), life for them must be confusing indeed!

Jovanny

"You start with a darkness to move through but sometimes
the darkness moves through you." —DEAN YOUNG

Jovanny, seated across the aisle from Mama on the Greyhound, worried about her. The loss of the new sister hurt, for sure, but

Mama seemed to be taking it harder than the children. Right now Daisy was entertaining Rory in the seat in front of her, and Gage, next to Jovanny with his elbow on the window-side chair arm and his head in his hand, stared glumly out the window at the passing sameness. Jovanny, though guardedly comfortable with this daddy figure—in his heart of hearts he longed to take the initiative of furthering a relationship—was for the time being alarmed by the man's off-putting aloofness, to the point of some discomfort in sitting next to him.

The seat next to Mama was vacant, and he saw his chance. Rising gingerly, fearful of disturbing Gage's contemplation, he made his way across the aisle to Mama's side. She appeared to be sleeping, curled up toward the window with her head on her folded coat, her back to him. Right now that broad back held an allure Jovanny found irresistible. For much of the rest of the trek northward he remained at his station, guarding Mama from harm and cold and appreciating the warm refuge of her back against his small face and body. The others seemed to intuit the rightness of leaving them together there.

Nadine

*"Autism: Where the 'randomness of life' collides
and clashes with an individual's need
for the sameness."* —EILEEN MILLER

The street that skirted the back of the neighborhood park ran in a semicircle, darkly outlined on the opposite side by one of those heavily wooded areas native to the locale—all pines. This unique lane had long ago grabbed Lannie's attention. Adele, thinking her asleep one evening in the car seat behind her, had been surprised when the little girl roused herself with the request, "Let's take the wiggle road, Nanna." The designation had caught on to the point that the family would deliberately "wiggle its way home" when time and opportunity meshed, even if it meant going slightly out of the way.

This designation had caught the fancy of Nadine too. Whether it was the "wiggle" or the woods Adele had never been able to determine, but that semicircular lane, tree-covered from the park side, belying its suburban location, seemed a world apart from the predictable, squared-off residential neighborhood, which Adele viewed as quintessentially American. Dog walkers, including Lauren and Adele, gravitated toward it, and children dreamed and imagined along its short route.

Adele had long ago given Nadine permission to visit the park on her own, designating the green bench at its close outskirts as the limit of these forays and stipulating that the wiggle road, and the small lake close to it, were off limits to her sister except when accompanied. Adele, able to glimpse the bench from the picture window, had over time developed confidence that this distinction had been internalized. Perhaps this allowance was less than prudent, but the liberty seemed to mean a great deal to Nadine. And Adele herself benefited from the break.

On this particular March morning the sixty-six year old, safeguarded by sensible winter gear thanks to her caregiver sister, in childish glee was making the block-long trek on her own for the first time since mid-autumn. Upon arrival Nadine announced companionably to the bench, "Here I am!" before settling down.

Daisy

"The day you stop being compassionate, your adjective of human drops!" —MEHMET MURAT ILDAN

"Morning, Vanessa."

"'Mornin', Mrs. Trumball."

"You'll never guess who's b-a-a-a-c-k!"

"Not our little Daisy?"

"In the flesh. Her mom's boyfriend evidently dropped the kids off this morning with very little explanation. No school information. Guess it's been an extended vacation."

"Quote unquote, right?"

"You've got it. Go a little easy on her. She seems a bit shell-shocked."

"I doubt I'll make much progress with her. Not much year left."

"I know. I'll ask Mrs. Graham to put her back in my room next year. Hopefully things will calm down by then, and she can use the extra time."

"You've got it. I'll be thrilled to see our kiddo!"

"She's a sweetie, all right. No matter how many years I put in I never get used to these midyear disappearances."

"Parkside sees enough of them. If they aren't getting evicted, they're running from the law or CPS or creditors or who knows what else?"

"Expect the unexpected, right?"

Lexie

"Nanna, sometimes I want you."

Lexie, who could be painfully shy in public, had picked up a bevy of imaginary friends. Adele had tried one Sunday morning to capitalize on this by suggesting that her granddaughter invite one of her "girls" to Sunday school. Lexie chose Pluto (yes, her girl's name was Pluto), and while the four year old didn't participate in class verbally, the teacher reported that she did at least participate.

Looking back, the fall months in preschool had been a difficult transition. Though Lexie had never complained about going, she had shrunk back in class till around mid-October, mouthing her first words at that time, to the surprise of Miss Tish and Miss Celine, who had wondered between themselves whether Lexie might be "slow." The little girl's first words, which had taken everyone aback, had been in response to a trinket she had brought from home catching the attention of a tablemate. Lexie's protest—"That's mine!"—had launched her as a contributing member of the group. And her budding friendship with

Haley had done much since then to offset the slow start.

This afternoon Adele lay down with Lexie for a nap. The little girl was active for several minutes in preparation for relaxation but eventually quieted, her little hand reaching over to touch Nanna's arm and her toes exploring beneath the light throw to feel her leg. Lexie's breathing deepened simultaneously with those confirming touches and soon enough steadied in sleep. Waiting a couple of minutes to make certain, Adele eased herself from the bed to check on Luke and Nadine. The little girl emerged from the bedroom only minutes later. When Adele commented that her nap had been short, she agreed: "I got up because I couldn't feel you anymore."

The comforting presence both of Adele and of Lauren in Lexie's life made all the difference for this vulnerable second child, so different in temperament from her dauntless sister. Lexie's sensitivity was acute, putting her at continuous risk of insecurity. She craved reassurance; her survival hinged on taking the risk to reach out and depend. While the self-assured Lannie at times needed reeling in, Lexie required continual nudges, pep talks, and reinforcement.

Adele recognized that to love is to risk a lack of reciprocation—no small matter for a child like Lexie. We who are more sophisticated and less dependent, she reflected, are more inclined to weigh the pros and cons before giving of ourselves wholly in a relationship. Perhaps Adele needed to ask herself a new question: *If I weren't so sure of God, how badly would I want him?* Tangentially, a related question confronted her: How badly does *Lauren* want him . . . ?

Lexie, this second daughter, was something of an enigma to Lauren, who as the youngest in her own family had inherited self-assurance from the encouragement of four siblings. Roddy and Adele had raised their tail-ender differently from the others, not giving in to her whims but in some sense indulging their own ability to hone in on the needs and promise of one rather than five, or four within close age range.

Mallory

*"In a world gushing blood day and night, you
never stop mopping up pain."* —ABERJHANI

Mallory was hemorrhaging, physically and emotionally. Had there been within her experience appreciable spiritual substance, that would undoubtedly have bled too. The night came when an ambulance arrived at the hotel and parked in front of room 222. Curious residents peered from behind almost-closed drapes; the revolving red strobe had awakened them like an insistent, thrumming heartbeat. It took nearly half an hour before the gurney emerged, the blond strands of hair revealing the prone form to be hers. More than another thirty minutes passed before the cab arrived for the man and children, the smallest too groggy to make the short walk without being scooped up into his arms. Excitement over, the unseen audience drifted back, one or two at a time, to bed and/or sleep. She returned by cab two days later, wan and tight-lipped, accompanied by the family.

Mallory's DNC stanched her physical flow, and she gradually learned to stifle the other. The four walls closing in on her in the dark weeks to follow, though, refused to allow the pain to dissipate. And the near-continuous presence of at least one little one within the constricting space allowed her no outlet for anguish.

Lannie

*"Why-why-why! . . . Ask it of everything your mind touches,
and let your mind touch everything!"* —ANN FAIRBAIRN

Adele, weary, permitted herself almost to drift off in the recliner—to venture into that middle level between alertness and slumber. Lauren was in class, and the creak of Nadine's rocker assured her of status quo in that area. The children played at her feet, in that close sibling proximity allowing for companionship with separate engagement, while Arabelle and Baby Girl reclined, also on the floor.

Lannie's stocking-footed departure from the room made no inroad into Adele's consciousness, and no one else remarked on it. Twenty minutes later the child padded back in, rivulets from a dripping head accompanying her progress. It was Nadine's barking laugh that awakened her sister.

"Nanna, did you know water turns hair brown?" Lannie asked innocently. And, indeed, her blonde tresses, now falling in tightly formed, dripping icicles, did appear darker. This was followed by a separate observation: "Water is invisible" [transparent, Adele guessed], "like gas."

Less than amused, Adele roused and raised herself with an audible sigh, followed immediately by an apology: "Sorry, Honey. I'm kindof at the end of my rope here this evening." *So like her mom*, she mused moments later as, Lannie's head over the kitchen sink, she rinsed out the liquid hand soap. Adele's tired resignation lifted slightly with the resumption of action. "You're laughing, Nanna," her granddaughter observed from her stooped position moments later. "You're getting towarder the top of your rope!"

Chuckling, Adele allowed her thought train to wander. When it came to technology, her youngest daughter was indeed the workaround queen extraordinaire. Alongside the living room entertainment center stood a tower of machines, with an Amazonian maze of cords looping to the floor behind it. Not having touched a DVD for some time, Adele had only a few evenings earlier been preparing to play a Disney movie for the kids. Avoiding both of the nonworking DVD players (one of which was built in to the aging set), she had slotted the disk into the second-to-the-top gaming device but was stumped from there—as was the usually proficient Lannie. A call to Lauren at work (she had traded her day shift hours with a coworker for the 3:00 to 11:00 shift) had yielded the less than helpful instruction to "play with it."

It had been the following day before Adele knew (not by virtue of playing but through explicit instruction) that she had to switch out the three color-coded wires leading to the TV (if the topmost gaming device had been in use), set the TV to AV2, and at the "play" prompt hit "X" on the controller for the second gaming device. Lest she forget, Adele had painstakingly written all of this down, while Lannie, the methodical, quietly absorbed it at her side.

It's funny the ways in which we depend on each other, Adele reflected now, toweling Lannie's head. The day-to-day interactions of a family take place in myriad small, but often seemingly indispensable ways.

Grant

" . . . the air seem[ed] to gather around her like held breath. As if this whole place were a story about her." —LAINI TAYLOR

There she was again. Grant had taken to sitting in the last seat of the last row of desks for his Tuesday evening pre-calculus class just to keep her in sight. She was pretty in her own way—not perky or pert, exactly (she was a little too tall for that)—but captivating to him in both looks and mannerisms, a willowy brunette with soft, shoulder-length curls, soft brown eyes, and a soft, dimpled smile—yes, *soft* was the word. Not altogether, though. She had a presence about her, an understated confidence. Lauren wasn't a still-life kind of pretty girl but one whose carriage, mannerisms, and gestures completed a package. It was difficult to calculate her age, though he would guess early thirties, like himself.

Grant hadn't been shy in getting to know her, though he hadn't yet singled her out from the group either. The three-hour class included a break in which classmates shared coffee and chitchat. Like Grant, Lauren expressed an interest in architecture, but he found himself charmed by her ambivalence on the subject. While artistically inclined and interested in both the beauty and the strength of well-constructed buildings, Lauren valued untouched land and hated urban sprawl.

In all honesty, he couldn't say she had betrayed any reciprocal interest, though she was invariably friendly. It hadn't taken a long time of standing in the hallway for him to determine that he was slightly shorter than she. Grant assessed himself—objectively, he thought—as being nondescript, serious and average with his carefully groomed brown hair and glasses. Never married, he was a slow mover in terms of the dating scene. He knew what he wanted, though, and asking out this girl was definitely a possibility.

Arabelle

"Doors to beautiful things do not remain open forever.
Be fast to enter inside!" —MEHMET MURAT ILDAN

Lauren, cross-legged on the living room floor surrounded by her three, dropped a dog treat through the rear bars of Arabelle's unoccupied but open crate. Arabelle, from the outside, attempted to access the morsel, slipping first one paw and then the other through the rear bars and then attempting to maneuver the goodie closer by shifting the portable crate floor. It never occurred to her to run to the other side and enter through the door.

Adele

"It's spring fever. . . . And when you've got it,
you want—oh, you don't quite know what it is you
do want, but it just fairly makes your heart
ache, you want it so!" —MARK TWAIN

"Nanna," Lexie asked, preparing to climb into bed, "How big's the temp'ature?"

"It's about 38."

"Wow! That's a lot of degrees."

Well, conceded Adele to herself, *it is and it isn't.* If any month of the year tended to try her patience, it was March. She didn't expect anything but inclement weather in January and February (*Was there such a thing as "clement" weather?*). But the *prospect of* the *possibility* of warmth tickled her fancy enough to make the continuing cold of March, and some years even of April, seem interminable. She'd just this evening bristled when the weatherman had predicted temps in the thirties for the entire eight-day forecast. It was technically spring, or as good as. And at this time of year she wanted more than anything else to get technical and hold the reality to it.

The extended "dead" time of late winter gave her the feeling of being all revved up with nowhere to go. Of experiencing an adrenaline rush for no apparent reason long about bedtime, only to rise hours later to the promise of another day of same old same old. What was she to do with this unchanneled energy? Lie awake half the night, first counting the hours till morning and finally (when she remembered having nothing in the near future to be excited about) switching to a tally of the hours of missed sleep? And then, like tonight, barely getting the kids in bed before feeling the need to turn in herself? All people, she guessed, pine for fulfillment, for closure, for "it" to be buttoned up and beautiful—whatever "it" is. Whether the issue was a disappointing eight-day forecast or a season of life that had begun to drag— it helped to know and believe God had better things in store!

It was at this point that Adele checked herself. Once in a while a more ruthlessly realistic train of self-talk surprised her, betrayed her, even, by calling into question the cheerfulness she had long taken for granted. It was at such times that Adele wondered whether her optimism functioned as a veneer to trivialize less welcome, more confusing emotions. Was it easier to face life convinced that positivity was her trademark? Had she somewhere along the line adopted that characteristic as a convenient coping mechanism? Why, Adele wondered now, did she find it so hard to admit that her life *wasn't* always good or easy or comfortable? Was her hopefulness a matter of pride, a façade she could present to a world—perhaps in particular to the Christians in her world—to ensure admiration for her spunk and determination against some difficult odds?

Self-recognition came hard to Adele, and she had become good over the years at dismissing such moments of acknowledgment as quickly as possible. Adele recognized now, as she seldom did, an undercurrent within her that felt more like depression than happiness.

Rory

> *"You could hold me and I could hold you. And it would*
> *be so peaceful. Completely peaceful. Like the feeling*
> *of sleep, but awake in it together."* —JOHN GREEN

More than ever the two year old missed his brother and sister during those long hours when they were away at school. Mama had in the past usually attempted to keep him occupied, if not in activity then in conversation. Now for the most part morning cartoons had taken over both roles. Though accustomed to this brand of entertainment, he found it lacking in the companionship he craved. Periodically during those hours Rory would sidle up to Mama or snuggle next to her on the bed (she was there now more than ever). Despite her responses—hugs and distant smiles—though, she seemed uninvolved, in a world as far away from Rory, *personally*, as life's TV version. The boy longed during those hours for a friend, a playmate, a confidante, though it would have been difficult for him to express confidences—or feel confident. The life and reality he had "always" taken for granted now baffled him at a deep level.

Lauren

> *"There's many a forward look in a backward glance."*
> —AUTHOR UNKNOWN

En route home from her Tuesday evening class, Lauren swung in to the bank lot to withdraw a twenty from the ATM. As she reached toward the screen she inadvertently touched it (evidently in the $400 fast-cash box), producing a dutiful response from the machine, which shot out twenty twenties (rarely available but re-cently deposited—part paycheck and part bonus). Methodically re-depositing all but one, the thirty-two year old couldn't help but gloat over her success. The growth was slow, yes, but cred-its were accumulating in terms both of her academic record and of her modest account and upwardly mobile credit score. Only two years earlier, adjusting to an unexpected reality and saddled with three preschoolers, her future had seemed a hopeless uphill climb. Had she overreacted to Gage's drunken assault—his *one* and *only* time? Lauren resisted recalling her own stridently preg-nant provocation on that night. But no, there'd been no excuse for that fist to the face, no matter how irrational her tirade.

At this quiet moment—it occurred to Lauren that the car radio was off—hindsight was speaking loudly. Who would have thought only two plus years earlier that those nineteen twenties that had just slipped through her fingers would *still be her own and at her disposal*—not exactly discretionary income but hers to apply to her modest monthly bills? Life with Mom and Aunt Na-dine, if anything, seemed more tolerable today than it had twelve years earlier, when Lauren had been a lovesick, champing-at-the-bit twenty year old in mostly unspoken opposition to her mom and soon-to-be-ailing dad. Adele's presence in the current picture more than resolved what would otherwise prove a nearly insur-mountable babysitting dilemma; she knew from the situations of coworkers how difficult it was to fork over precious paycheck dol-lars for childcare—hardly making it worthwhile for them to work.

Despite everything, though, Lauren had loved Gage. Those initial five years of care- and child-freedom had been an unforget-table hiatus from responsibility—if you could legitimately take a hiatus at the frontend . . . The happy vagabonds had needed little and been contented with less, to the point that survival had at times seemed a dare. The trouble had come when responsibility finally *did* stare them in the face and Gage, drinking heavily, had failed to rise to the occasion. On a financial level she was defi-nitely better off without him and his habit.

Lauren, though totally over Gage, still liked him—his lanky blonde good looks and good humor, his innate sensitivity and—she had to admit it—his affinity with kids. Gage had given her more than a decade of good years, counting the before-marriage relationship, but good looked different now to a thirty-something, finally-coming-of-age mom, employee, and student. Lauren conceded with a grin she couldn't stifle that life had never looked more promising.

Adele's Devotion: A March Reading

BETWEEN GRACES

"The desert and the parched land will be glad; the wilderness will rejoice and blossom. Like the crocus, it will burst into bloom." (ISAIAH 35:1–2)

Here in the Midwest the crocus is an early harbinger of spring. This hardy, often sun-hued flower can sustain some weather reversals, but unseasonal balmy weather can coax out its blossoms prematurely. As any Midwesterner can attest, springtime in this part of the world comes in fits and starts—including some false starts.

Charles Dickens describes this in-between time with precision: "It was one of those March days when the sun shines hot and the wind blows cold: when it is summer in the light, and winter in the shade." Or, in the words of poet Lilja Rogers,

> *"First a howling blizzard woke us,*
> *Then the rain came down to soak us,*
> *And now before the eye can focus—*
> *Crocus."*

Isaiah in the verses above was describing a day in which there will be no unsung natural catastrophes or human ca-

sualties. I appreciate Nathaniel Hawthorne's take on this issue: "Our Creator would never have made such lovely days, and have given us the deep hearts to enjoy them, . . . unless we were meant to be immortal."

April

Adele

*"Quite a lot of our contemporary culture
is actually shot through with a resentment of limits and
the passage of time, anger at what we can't do, fear or
even disgust at growing old."* —ROWAN WILLIAMS

While Adele tended to push speed limits when she could get away with it, the surprise following a locally raised speed limit affecting several east-west arteries was that she found it hard to keep up with the higher threshold. "Flying" along at seven or eight miles above the previously posted limit, she realized that she could legitimately go faster. Her exhilaration at this lack of restriction was almost laughable. Yet it seemed as though she had to concentrate to push the pedal hard enough to maintain a reasonable five miles over the limit.

The truth was, Adele realized, that she resented limitations. She had long functioned on an unspoken premise of being above them. Not above the law—that wasn't the issue at all—but above those human, physical restrictions that affected other people. For most of her adult life Adele had considered herself something of an automaton, in some unrealistic and ridiculous sense unaffected by those factors that acted as a drag on others.

It had been a while since she'd actually entertained such thoughts. There could be no doubt now, at sixty-three, that internal speed limits were coming into play. The reality, beyond being a nuisance, felt diminishing and at times a betrayal. The future that had always seemed so open-ended, even in terms of her earthly life, seemed to be closing in on her. In terms of Lauren's children in particular, how hands-on could she continue to be into the next decade? And she'd be into her late seventies by the time they experienced the vigor of young adulthood.

There'd been no problem early on functioning as Grandma—for years side-by-side with Grandpa—with regard to the first set of grandchildren, the oldest of whom were already in or near their twenties, dating, in college, all of the usual milestones. How—and why—had Adele convinced herself that the role of surrogate mom was hers for the taking with Lauren's three little ones? Somewhere along the line her perspective had become skewed, and it wasn't fair to any of those involved, very much including Lauren and even herself. A course correction was unavoidable, even if she didn't have to face it quite yet . . .

Lannie

"[W]hat you learn today, for no reason at all,
will help you discover all the wonderful secrets
of tomorrow." —NORTON JUSTER

Lannie's use of household materials was frequently untraditional. If a product or texture reminded her of something else, she would, given half a chance, take the comparative initiative. Edibles and other consumables, as well as natural objects, frequently found usage in unusual and artistic ways. Experimentation with food was no exception. Here she was, crunching her baby-cut-carrot sandwich, one cheek swollen like a chipmunk.

Lannie herself broke the brief silence, despite the necessity of temporarily garbled speech, announcing matter-of-factly, "Nanna, we need new toothpaste."

"I thought I just bought you guys some."

"You did, but I useded it to make a picture of a muffin."

Adele, who hadn't seen that particular work of art, wondered

When? and, more particularly, *Where . . . had the little girl stashed this masterpiece?*

Gage

*"Of course God does not consider you hopeless.
If He did, He would not be moving you to seek Him
(and He obviously is) . . . Continue seeking Him
with seriousness. Unless He wanted you, you
would not be wanting Him."* —C. S. LEWIS

Gage, accustomed by now to his unintentional sobriety, had also been sobered by the North Carolina experience to the point of serious reflection—and appreciation for what he still had. Appreciation, he acknowledged, with nowhere to lay it. God came to mind, certainly, but would God be interested even in that brand of prayer after what he, Gage, had just led this trusting family to do? Was he in any way responsible for the brevity of that angel life? That question would haunt him for a lifetime, he knew. Which was okay, just in case he deserved it. Gage allowed himself to dwell on God's mercy in bringing him back to his senses and all of them back home. *Maybe this kind of backhanded thanks—acknowledged internally if not voiced—would suit with God, who could read the heart, right?*

Despite the lack of an impressive employment history, Gage cleaned up and presented well. Little more than a month after the return he burst through the hotel room door, face flushed for an unaccustomed reason, to announce in real glee that he had landed a position at a rapid oil change location. Gage adapted well to the protocol and lingo—the coded working language in the customer's presence made him feel initiated and professional—and took pride in his uniform. More importantly, he began setting before his woman—as proud as a cat laying a bird at the master's feet—a modest paycheck.

Seeing his own children was becoming a compulsion, Gage knew. There was something about the life of that baby girl who had lived for hours (*Why hadn't he and Mallory thought to name her?*) that, though incomplete, tied everything together. This child whose life had been cut so short *had lived*, and lived long enough to . . . almost . . . make mutual siblings of the six remaining children in his life. In some strange way Mallory's three were becoming melded in Gage's mind through this shared half-sister with Alanna, Alexa, and Luke—that "other" little boy he himself had fathered but had never yet laid eyes on. Seeing his children—the other three—seemed strangely necessary for Gage's completion as a man, a lover, and a father. Someday he would let them know that their unnamed sister had lived for part of a night in a drafty old house without a furnace in North Carolina.

Gage was reminded, unaccountably, of the baby Jesus in the manger when the inn was full, though he wasn't quite sure of the legitimacy of the connection. Way back in the day when Lauren's dad, Roddy, had still lived, his own and Lauren's attendance at the Sunday morning service had been a given, at least for as long as she'd made her parents' home her own. Although the two of them hadn't continued this tradition during their vagabond years nor thought of it during those crazy days of drinking and preschoolers and irresponsibility and a troubled marriage, Gage had never minded church. Now he was becoming sentimental in his old age—or was it his sobriety?

The next obvious question was *Why not make contact with Lauren, asking her to reconsider the PPO—officially, through an attorney or the court, or whatever the protocol? Why not convince her that he had changed, that he was sober and learning responsibility, in love with a woman he had every intention of marrying and fast falling "in love" with her three beautiful children? What fear of refusal (or was it his unrelenting guilt?) so possessed him that he could only envision proceeding in the wrong way?* For the time being he wanted just one audience with his biological offspring. He owed them that. Was it really too much to ask—*If only he could bring himself to ask the Someone with the answer!*—now especially, after all he'd been through?

Lexie

*"Wonder can't be packaged, and it can't be
worked up. It requires some sense of being there
and some sense of engagement."*
—EUGENE H. PETERSON

She'd begun life as a two-and-a-half-foot-tall Kmart Easter bunny, purchased by Lauren on a whim as a spring spruce-up. But sometime during the course of a difficult year when Lexie was two, she had morphed into the little girl's "best friend" and inseparable companion. In the meantime she'd suffered serious deterioration, becoming the child's personal velveteen rabbit.

Then one day four-year-old Lexie forced Bunny's fused metal spine into a sitting position, and the skeleton snapped at the waist. "Is it time to introduce death?" Lauren wondered aloud to Adele, all the while fighting the notion. Tools in hand, Adele's resourceful daughter managed to drill new holes through the metal backbone cylinder, and a much shortened but still viable Bunny emerged. Bunny had experienced a resurrection.

Nadine

*"We know that [people] with autism like order,
that they are often very visual and that they can be
quite literal. They deserve beautiful resources and
symbols that make sense."* —ADELE DEVINE

"Look, Nanna." Lexie had emerged from church school this Palm Sunday morning, a colorful masterpiece clutched in her palm. "I made a cross. God died on a cross."

"Jesus did die on a cross for us," Adele confirmed. "And then what happened?"

"Then he went alive again."

Luke, to whom this news sounded impressive, paused to take a good look at his big sister's craft, Aunt Nadine at his side.

"Pretty," Nadine concluded, at which she raised both arms in an inclusive, all-encompassing gesture. "Jesus is *so* pretty!" Luke and Lexie nodded solemnly.

"Beautiful Savior!" came unbidden to Adele's mind. When Luke reached an age at which he could handle more information—Lexie and Lannie were already there—she couldn't fail to fill in the detail, simple as it was, and yet so profound. A line from another song familiar to the congregation played out in her mind: "How will they know unless we teach them so?"

> *"Deep within, there is something profoundly known, not consciously, but unconsciously. A quiet truth, that is not a version of something, but an original knowing. . . . It is so self-sustaining that our recognition of it is not required. We are [offspring] of such a powerfully divine force—Creator of all things known and unknown."* —T. F. HODGE

That knowing was so subjective with regard to the little ones, coming as it did so piecemeal and yet so adequate for each stage of comprehension. At bottom it was for all of them, including herself, a heart knowing—and hearts can know and accept on so many levels, all fully adequate in God's sight based on who and where the person is.

Adele had never entertained a doubt about her sister's faith, expressed as it was periodically and in quirky ways. Nadine had for all the years her younger sister had known her been entered into a love affair with God and Jesus—not that she consistently distinguished the Persons of the godhead or their roles. She knew little of the Holy Spirit, though she had expressed many times God's presence in her midriff area ("Don't punch my tummy; that's where Jesus is"). But the Spirit knew her, keeping her safe and pure and ready for that eventual day of departure.

Daisy

"Babies are such a nice way to start people."—DON HEROLD

Mrs. Jillian, Mrs. Trumball's first-semester aide, was coming to visit the classroom that morning with her month-old daughter.

Mrs. Trumball prepared the children; they would be permitted one by one to pass the chair in which Mrs. Jillian would sit, holding little Kylie, to greet the baby (no breathing directly on her, loud voices, kisses, or rough touches). Several of the children shared experiences with younger siblings in their own homes, babies now or in the not too distant past. The girls in particular, for the most part avid mamas-to-be, waited with nervous excitement; some of the boys seemed indifferent or uncertain.

When her turn arrived Daisy, wide-eyed and solemn, responded differently from the *oohing* and *aahing* little girls around her. Interested in spite of her pledge to herself to remain aloof, the little girl stood for a long moment, seeming more to study the baby than to admire her. Yielding to an unchecked impulse, she reached out a single finger and brushed it against the tiny, soft arm, starting as though deeply moved by the contact. Jillian smiled encouragingly, taking in her unreadable expression and asking how she was doing. Daisy, finding herself, reciprocated, her wide smile contrasted with puddled black eyes. "She's beautiful," she intoned. "You must *really* love her!"

Lauren

"This thing about you that you think is your flaw—
it's the reason I'm falling in love with you."
—COLLEEN HOOVER

The truth was that, for her part, Lauren *had* noticed Grant, primarily at first in contrast to Gage with his unruly good looks and adolescent swagger. The only eligible older guy in pre-calc, Grant appealed to her on the basis of both his sensibility and his sensitivity. Not a catch in terms of looks—not that he was deficient in any way—Grant caught her eye on the basis of his reliability and evident certainty about the direction of his life. It was funny how her criteria for a guy had changed over slightly more than a decade. Lauren wasn't smitten with Grant but liked him, allowing her thoughts to stray to the possibility of some outside social interaction. The semester would draw to a close in May, though, and he hadn't yet asked her out. Either way would be fine . . .

Luke

"Having a two-year-old is like having a blender that
you don't have the top for."—JERRY SEINFELD

Vrrroom. Eeert. Pow. Crash. Kaboom. Ggggrrroar. Wooo-oo-OOO. Keeping up with Luke had a full-time feel to it. The steady stream of highly inflected onomatopoetic noises emerging from his mouth, let alone his ever-moving body, could be unnerving. *How does Nanna manage?* Lauren wondered with true appreciation. There could be no doubt: raising a little boy was an altogether different proposition from the same general category of activity related to a toddler of the opposite gender. And it had been that way almost from her son's earliest days. Her little girls—Lexie more than Lannie—had at that age been all about murmurs and whispers and secrets and kisses, about gestures and choreography. Luke was too vital for choreographed movement, though his activity was incessant, at times verging on frenetic. And no one suggested hyperactivity—just "all boy," spoken with a satisfaction that sounded at times like a smug "It's your turn. How does it feel?"

Jovanny

"Memories are bullets. Some whiz by and only spook you. Others
tear you open and leave you in pieces." —RICHARD KADREY

Jovanny's return to the classroom gladdened Miss Gentry's heart. An effusive kindergarten teacher, she poured her all into her students and considered her vocation a labor of love. She noticed from the outset, though, that the black eyes that could flash so engagingly could also mask. While the little she knew of his background suggested that Jovanny's lot was less than ideal, this shuttered closeness was alarming in one so young. Mrs. Graham had little knowledge of what had gone on during the family's absence—other than the fact that schooling had evidently not been a part of it—and Miss Torne, the social worker, was unauthorized to probe without parental request, or at least consent, which was unlikely to be forthcoming. Anyway, Miss Gentry could pinpoint no specific problem; Jovanny participated as he always had—almost as though no intermission had punctuated his routine. Still, there was something there, or some spark no longer there, that disturbed her.

The situation changed on the morning she asked the boys and girls to draw pictures of their families. Jovanny's included a tall, yellow-haired man and a shorter woman of the same coloration—both smiling—along with three brown-skinned, black-haired children, the shortest with corkscrew curls. In typical kindergarten fashion, a brown line indicated ground level, and a yellow-haired baby with no visible eyes (closed?) lay beneath the line, surrounded by a brown circle. In front of the family on the ground? Or under that ground?

When Miss Gentry nonchalantly sought clarification on this point, the little boy burst into tears. After he had been calmed, a meeting ensued with Jovanny, Miss Gentry, Mrs. Graham, Miss Torne, and a female police officer, after which Daisy was called upon to collaborate and expand upon what they'd been able to glean from her brother.

Mallory

"It has been my experience that guilt can burst through the smallest breach and cover the landscape, and abide in it in pools and danknesses, just as native as water."—MARILYNNE ROBINSON

The detective with whom Gage and Mallory met, also a female, was far from unkind or insensitive. Though it was necessary for the two of them to interview in an interrogation room at the police department—much better, Mallory recognized, than sitting at the foot of a hotel bed, and much less conducive to gossip—the woman accommodated the mother's lack of a babysitter for her two year old, allowing him to sit on her lap or play at her feet during the conversation.

Although there was no suggestion or evidence at this point that a crime had been committed, she gave the couple to understand that it would be necessary to exhume the body for investigation. At this mention a shockwave ran through Mallory to the point that she shuddered and grabbed Gage's knee for support. This could, she recognized later, have been viewed as a guilt reaction, but it wasn't—wasn't such and evidently wasn't construed that way. The detective offered to supply a glass of water, which Mallory declined, and then waited discreetly for the mother to compose herself.

This outcome came as no surprise, really—*What else could either of them have expected?* It was the horror of the thought that ran through the mother like a hot knife. The little girl had been laid to rest an angel, never in Mallory's mind to be disturbed in her shallow resting place. In fact, she had taken special care not to mess with that knowledge, not to allow a conscious thought to so much as brush up against it. Now to her horror she pictured skeletal remains in the cardboard box. *Would the little outfit be ragged, dirty, or wet?* Why this detail disturbed her she couldn't have explained, but it seemed important, not in terms of mitigating her guilt but in honor of the brief life she'd been too ill and exhausted to cherish, indeed even to acknowledge beyond that initial attempt at nursing.

The truth was that Mallory had spent a lifetime not simply exposed to shame but immersed in it. She and Gage may not have been directly responsible for the child's passing, but she was to blame on so many levels—for having become pregnant, given the circumstances; for having allowed the situation to become so dire; for having failed to name this daughter or even to dignify her death by contacting the police—not that the family had been in possession of a phone or, by that point, a running car. Mallory's shame, truth be told, seemed to go all the way back to her own conception and birth. It hadn't taken long in the girl's young life for her to *be-*

come shame, to take it upon herself as her due and identity.

Now the thought of a perceived allegation was unbearable. *Was this why so many deeply shamed people so readily confessed to crimes that hadn't been theirs to commit?* What a relief it would be at this very moment to blurt out a full confession, embellishing it in any way possible to ensure a swift and final consequence. Mallory's rational mind played a tape suggesting that she and Gage had done—without consultation with one another, even— only what had seemed at the moment appropriate or, more to the point, possible. Perhaps in the long run the knowledge that the brief life was to be dignified—implied to have mattered, based on an after-the-fact investigation of the death, along with a proper burial—would become meaningful—even (*dare she think it?*) a source of some comfort.

Rory

"The distinction between children and adults, while probably useful for some purposes, is at bottom a specious one, I feel. There are only individual egos, crazy for love." —NICCOLO MACHIAVELLI

Rory understood bits and pieces of the conversation in the little room with no windows and a closed door—very likely more than the three adults would have given him credit for. His recall of the days they were discussing was razor sharp; Rory noticed things and hung on to them for further mulling. Sensing the reticence of both of the adults in his life, he had forced himself ever since to remain mum, though a lengthening list of questions was thrusting hard from the inside to be let out. Now, at long last listening to words from all three adults pertaining to this pivotal point in his two-year-old life, he was all ears without letting on.

At last, overloaded—the discussion was droning on far too long—he crawled into Gage's lap; wrapped his arms around his neck, snuggling in to that comfortable crevice just below the chin; felt Gage's answering embrace; and gave in to weariness. Rory's blue eyes fluttered open and shut a few times, catching an approving smile on the lips of the uniformed officer. The lady liked that he hadn't been naughty. All the rest would make more sense after his nap . . .

At some point the grace of advancing age would expunge from the toddler's conscious memory bank the cameos of that "other" sister, but the life-learnings would remain forever a part of Rory the boy, and eventually of Rory the man.

Adele's Devotion: An April Reading

OUTPOURING

"He poured out his life unto death, and was numbered with the transgressors." (ISAIAH 53:12)

I'm moved by the image of Jesus pouring out his life. On the one hand I visualize an outflow of lifeblood—a poignant, passive image, a being poured out. Yet on a deeper level I see spilling over a love too thrusting to be contained—the definition of proactivity, a voluntary pouring out. Yes, Jesus obeyed the Father, but the decision to sacrifice himself was his own.

The only appropriate response to such love will be voluntary and insistent too. When have you experienced a love so overwhelming you could neither squelch it nor hold it in? A gratitude so urgent you just had to pass it on? That's the impetus of the Christian faith, an unstoppable momentum to spread an unquenchable love.

May

Grant

"Good communication is as stimulating
as black coffee and just as hard to sleep after."
—ANNE MORROW LINDBERGH

It was soon to be now or never. The semester would draw to a close in three short weeks, and Lauren had done nothing to snub or disappoint him. Grant wasn't shy—just careful—and he had decided during the previous week that he would follow through this evening, provided she was in class.

She was—not that she had missed a single one so far. It wasn't difficult during the break to draw her aside (informal little groups dotted the hallway outside the door). This was the first time the two had spoken privately, and a comfort level was evident from both sides. Lauren was open about her personal circumstances, mentioning without detail her divorce after nine mostly good years, her current residence with her mom and aunt, her job at the hotel, and—finally and a little cautiously—her three lovely kids.

The vibes were good from Grant's perspective. Lauren evidently had nothing to hide, and her availability and possible interest came as a relief. Grant for his part loved children, having been raised oldest in an expanding family of them—preacher's kids (he preferred to think of himself as a pastor's son)—and foresaw no problem with a ready-made family at his age. He was jumping way ahead and knew it, but Grant was the type to weigh options at an early stage before proceeding with anything.

The moment was ripe for an invitation to get together for coffee, which Lauren readily accepted—she had hoped it would come. This would be her first date since Gage two-and-a-half years earlier, and the idea of a pleasant couple of hours at a coffee shop was welcome. She determined immediately that from her side there would be no holds barred. She was in a good position in life with no felt need for change; if there were evidence from his side of any red flags about her life she would chalk up the experience to an evening out and move on.

Rory

"Kids: they dance before they learn there is anything that isn't music." —WILLIAM STAFFORD

"Whatcha doin', little man?"

"*Dancing!* Wheee!" Rory wended his wavy way between the double beds, bumping and thumping as hips or outstretched hands made contact with one bed or the other.

"I don't hear any music."

"*I* do!"

"Well all right, then." Mallory, slowly reemerging into the stream of daily living, scooped up her son, plopped him on the bed, and commenced his favorite, "tickle torture."

"Shall we sit outside and watch the trucks go by?"

"Yeah!"

Moments later mother and son had settled themselves on the curb three steps from the door, Rory in parade mood. The scenery didn't quite match the mountain, and he missed *Him*, the limbless doll. But running fingers across the peaks of four knees—two mountaintops and the others foothills—served for the time being. The spring day was bright, and the combination of outside and Mama-love felt like the epitome of all things fine!

Nadine

"Disability is a matter of perception. If you can do just one thing well, you're needed by someone." —MARTINA NAVRATILOVA

Nadine's mentor at the church's Thursday evening gathering for disabled adults, most transported to the ministry center weekly from residential homes within the community, had been assigned two "friends"—the same welcoming designation officially used of classmates at Daisy and Jovanny's elementary school. Nadine and Caroline were both within a decade or so of Vicki's own age, and she felt she had by the end of the season made inroads in getting to know them both. Vicki found Nadine engaging—eager, funny, and knowledgeable about Bible stories and concepts. Whether touching base before the meeting, singing to rhythm instruments, applauding soloists (including those limited to unintelligible noises), sharing prayer requests, reenacting Bible stories, or working on crafts, Nadine participated with intensity and evident enjoyment.

In many ways her foil, the wheelchair-bound Caroline (of comparable mental ability and communication skills, though much less capable physically), approached the situation with reservation. She was opinionated in every way, ultrasensitive to lights too glaring or noises too blaring. Caroline invariably expressed excitement, though, when Vicki wore "blocks" (a sweater with a geometric pattern), and when something struck her as funny her chortles were heartfelt. She was never without a plush snake around her neck to ward off bugs or rowdy friends. Both Nadine and Caroline loved hymns and gospel songs. Caroline in particular recalled and shared with Vicki the context of when and how she had come to learn the lyrics for each one.

Vicki realized at this evening's celebration (cake and Bingo following the song session, prayer, and story), the season's "finale" before the summer break, that she would miss her friends over the three months. Despite their distinctive differences, each had found a place in her heart during this first year of acquaintance.

Jovanny

*"A child seldom needs a good talking
to as a good listening to."* —ROBERT BRAULT

Indoor recess on a rainy day. The kindergarten room was well equipped; Miss Gentry had in reserve stashes of special toys for just this situation. Jovanny, joined by a group of three, busied himself stacking plastic cups at a furious rate of speed, pouncing with his pile on one after another (manual dexterity in Miss Gentry's mind, fun in theirs). Seeing his opportunity a little later, though, he left his station, took a few tentative steps to the reading table where Miss Gentry sat, and sidled up to her. Seeing *her* opportunity, she wrapped her arm around him with a "What's up?" encouraging smile.

Jovanny had nothing serious to discuss that morning, but the listening ear of a welcoming grownup held its own allure. Moments later Miss Gentry could be heard chuckling softly in response to his pronouncement "Turtles love me. They just sit on my arm and purr!"

Adele

*"People stagger, but they pick up a tattered thread
and wind it back onto a spool."* —DONIA BIJAN

Waiting at the bank's drive-through window, Adele found herself captivated by the determination of a sparrow in the process of building a nest in the flat, recessed area above a light protruding from the side of the building. In the process of rearranging her twigs, grasses, and other materials, most of which were already intertwined, she would knock some of them over the lip, down to the ground below. Dropping almost straight down, she would grasp in her beak one twig from the tangle (hopefully all or most of it would remain intact), fly to a ledge approximately halfway up to the light fixture and to the right, change direction, and return with her clump to the construction site.

She would knock down much, if not all, of the same entwined thatch, only to dive-bomb once again to retrieve it, this time perhaps returning with only a disengaged twig. Adele watched this a few times before reaching the front of the line of cars, impressed by the bird mom's resolve, not to mention her lack of self-consciousness in spite of her captive audience. If discouraged by these repeated setbacks, she didn't show it.

"Do you want to cash or deposit that?"

"Oh, sorry, I was watching the bird building its next."

"Everybody says that," the teller responded with a smile. "I can't quite see it from here, but it's back every year."

Pulling away, Adele's thoughts ran to a song she had learned some sixty years earlier at her mother's knee. For most of the way home the simple lyrics played over and over in her mind: "God sees the little sparrow fall, It meets His tender view; If God so loves the little birds, I know He loves me too."

Daisy

"We worry about what a child will become tomorrow,
yet we forget that [she] is someone today." —STACIA TAUSHER

Daisy's early interest in design (revealed in part by her fascination with the large classroom dollhouse from Mrs. Trumball's own girlhood) had become apparent both to Mrs. Trumball and (in a different way) her art teacher. Several of the girls had declared themselves in one way or another "beyond" the doll stage (how sad, Mrs. Trumball couldn't help but reflect, for six year olds!), while the interests of others ran in different directions. This left Daisy and one or two other of the shyer, more sensitive girls to gravitate toward the dollhouse corner during indoor recess.

The play, when Daisy was involved, tended to be parallel, although the little girl, unfailingly courteous, responded to input from other girls. This child who, the teacher knew, made her home in a furnished hotel room, couldn't get enough of the allure of options. Given half a chance, she would become the type who would incessantly go after the new look, not in terms of fashion or décor as such but in the rearrangement of whatever was available for optimal effect. Mrs. Trumball sincerely hoped it wouldn't be long before Daisy's circumstances allowed her freer rein for self-expression.

Mallory

"I always feel sad for the girl I was,
because it never occurred to me that my mother
might comfort me. She has never told me she loved me,
and I never assumed she did. She tended to me.
She administered me." —GILLIAN FLYNN

Like Gage, Mallory had some prior experience with religion. But not like his. The God Mallory had known (*of*, that was) had, like Gage's, been all-knowing and all-powerful. He was also vindictive, manipulative, and sadistic, particularly when it came to little girls not prone to compliance. And for whatever reason Mallory hadn't always been submissive, particularly not as she'd grown a little older. Looking back now with a degree of objectivity, she recognized that this inborn spunk had largely been responsible for her survival.

Gage's take on God baffled her. The God he'd known was altogether different in character—a friend, a lover even. A Being for whom even forgiveness might not be out of the question, though Gage wasn't ready to believe right now that he was anywhere close to qualifying, particularly not *after* . . . Still, she was aware that he was dancing continually around that theme, not daring to risk an advance but wanting to.

Mallory found herself intrigued by the concept of approaching God, as opposed to running away. She hadn't the foggiest notion how one might make oneself available to such a deity but found herself wishing he were real. The other, passive course, which seemed to require no know-how, Mallory intuited as more feasible. If she—or Gage, for that matter—lacked the daring or felt entitlement to approach God, perhaps they could wait for him to take the initiative. Live right and hope or wish or imagine his sight could penetrate the darkness around and within them. To that Mallory was guardedly open, despite entrenched misgivings. At this point, what had she or Gage to lose?

Lexie

"Right is absence of wrongness and wrong is what seems to be unfair." —M. F. MOONZAGER

Lexie's kindergarten physical marked her first pediatrician visit in some time. Adele, who took her during Lauren's work shift, appreciated her granddaughter's perspectives on the situation. The workings of those active little minds never failed to fascinate their nanna. Despite being uninformed, Adele reflected, the children's logical thought processes were intact and, in their own precious way, remarkably insightful.

The visit began with the usual check of weight and height. Lexie, waiting till she was alone with Nanna, confided by way of explanation, "If I don't take off my shoes, the scale can't feel me." Minutes later, in the bathroom with Adele to "pee in the cup," she expressed curiosity about the purpose of this strange exercise: "Why does he need to check my water pressure?"

It was near the end of the visit that the nurse violated Lexie's trust by stabbing her without forewarning in the thigh (no doubt attempting to prepare a child for an inoculation, Adele recognized, would be futile, though this alternative approach seemed insensitive). As soon as Lexie's astonished screams punctuated the temporary silence of the corridor of pediatric examination rooms, the nurse jabbed her again, this time in the other thigh.

Vaccinations accomplished, Adele thought ruefully, but at what cost in terms of this sensitive child's future cooperation in a doctor's office? *Life isn't always fair,* she acknowledged with a wry half smile, watching her granddaughter moments later immersed in selecting a toy from the offered basket.

Gage

"Sometimes the greatest difference between being a boy and being a man is restraint." —DAVE DONOVAN

The interrogation, as Gage viewed it, had been a step beyond his tolerance boundaries. He had fought himself in the two plus weeks since that time but still found himself waiting for some invisible guillotine to drop. *No news might be good news*, he assured himself, but the suspense was proving more overwhelming than the recollections the investigation refused to let him sidestep. A part of Gage was angry at little Jovanny for opening the can of worms—*no, that image was all wrong!*—while at the same time he understood the inner thrust that must have impelled the five year old to vent some of the pressure by releasing a hint. Perhaps it was for the best. Though Gage had managed for nearly three months to squelch his intractable thoughts, the memory would eventually have caught up with him. Perhaps now, or soon, it could be laid to rest along with the child's remains.

Luke

"The cross is God taking on flesh and blood and saying, 'Me too.'" —ROB BELL

"Did bees sting God?" Luke asked nonchalantly, sitting on the porch steps a few feet removed from Adele and Nadine on their Adirondack chairs. He wielded a stick, with which he was making squiggles on the step beneath his feet. The May noontime was splendid, the epitome of loveliness as far as Adele was concerned. The garden was as manicured as it was likely to be; the warmer, dryer days to come would reduce her incentive, tending to drive her indoors once the sun beat down. The east-facing veranda limited the cooler morning time she considered prime for outdoor work.

"Good question, Luker," Adele responded. "Bees don't sting God in heaven, but they might have stung Jesus here on Earth.

Jesus is God and a man too. I bet he even got sick sometimes!" Probably too complicated a response, she recognized. A little went a long way with Luke, and much depended on the purpose behind his question.

This time the tot wrinkled his brow slightly, responding with only an "Oh!" For a short time he sat silent, deep in thought. *Reconsidering his theological framework*, Adele guessed with the hint of a smile.

Lauren

*"Worry not that your child listens to you; worry most
that they watch you."* —RONALD A. HEIFETZ

Near the school's front entrance on her day off to pick up Lannie for a dental appointment, Lauren watched the procession of thirty plus kindergarteners from Mrs. Davies's class trudging through the hallway, destination lunch, in a wavy, oft-broken thread. The line would continue until one child became diverted, turning around—which seemed to necessitate stopping—to interact with the next. Those behind the break would patiently wait until the aide called out to keep the line moving. This enterprising older lady had adopted an effective tactic. Lifting both arms as though in praise, she wiggled her fingers and waved her arms, followed by a mostly unbroken line of captivated little ones, those closest to the front following suit. The pied piper of Parkside.

Lannie

*"Memories of childhood were the dreams that stayed
with you after you woke."* —JULIAN BARNES

A three-generational Saturday-morning mother-daughter "tea" at church had drawn Adele and Lannie, with Lauren, less comfortable in light of her awkward string of absences, consenting to participate for her daughter's sake. Lexie and Luke were excited about visiting a babysitter with children of approximately their ages, and a friend was keeping Nadine company. Lannie flaunted her floral spring sundress, frilly socks, sandals, and hair ribbon. *How long will she be willing to accept the adorable little girl look?* Adele wondered, knowing on the other hand that this would be no problem for the whimsical Lexie for some time to come. Adele and Lauren for Lannie's sake dressed in kind, despite Lauren's usual overriding criterion of comfort. Adele shared her granddaughters' liking for all things pretty and delighted Lannie by selected a dressy pant with an attractive pastel blouse.

The morning's activities included painting miniature wooden birdhouses (in washable watercolors), followed by a sampling of teacakes, pastries, and assorted finger foods and beverages. A friend snapped their three-generational photo on Lauren's cell phone camera—each was holding her birdhouse. The special occasion with Momma *and* Nanna seemed to mean a great deal to the exuberant six year old, and the photo, later printed and enlarged for the mantle, would retain a place in the memory banks of all three.

Adele's Devotion: A May Reading

UNLIKELY GRACE

"'What is impossible with man is possible with God.'" (LUKE 1:37)

The natural world is replete with impossible, unnatural graces, with flickers of life that insist against all odds on having their day in the sun. Nineteenth-century English poet Dorothy Wordsworth commented on one such incongruity: "I found a strawberry blossom in a rock. I uprooted it rashly and felt as if I had been committing an outrage, so I planted it again." Life is incredibly opportunistic and optimistic, often triumphing in snatches of grace we view as altogether unlikely. The month of May showcases many of these brave forays, as does the human medical record.

We've grown so accustomed to salvation that we no longer view it as astonishing. But prior to the unfolding of God's "extended" life plan, who would have dared conjecture so outrageous a wonder? There's a sense in which all grace is startling. How incredible that the Creator of all, the God of the impossible, is also the God of grace!

June

Lannie

"Nanna, how do mushrooms get planted?"
"How does electricity get in lightning?"
"My nose bleeds when my vines get dry and snap."

*"You cannot catch a child's spirit by running after it; you must
stand still and for love it will soon itself return."* —ARTHUR MILLER

A broom-wielding Adele smiled appreciatively in response
to those bonus mini seasons, in terms of output from the sky,
punctuating the area in May and June. Long about mid May, as
though on cue, the neighborhood had been infiltrated by a perfect storm of maple-tree whirlybirds, reminding her of thousands
of little parachutists landing from hovering copters. Arabelle had
loved nothing better than to chase and pounce as the wind carried and then dropped phalanxes of these intruders in sudden,
lurching swirls.

There'd been no reprieve this year before the cottonwoods
had become active, coordinating with the wind to blow white
fuzzies into the yard until the junction of lawn and driveway
looked, as now, like the beginnings of a snowdrift. The small
lake a block away at the park, she'd noticed, had become covered
with these weightless floaties, its surface looking like a tabletop
in need of dusting. The winds were wasteful in terms of scatter-
ing nature's seed, but scatter it they did.

Still in an expansive frame of mind, her eye on the children playing in the far corner of her peripheral vision (Nadine, holding her dog-eared bird book, was established in her chair on the porch), she chuckled at the thought of their dealings with delight. Just minutes earlier Lannie of the sky's-the-limit capacity for wonder had demonstrated her disarming lack of distinction between perceived and imagined marvels. Some of her hypotheses were easy enough to see through: "My taste bugs can't taste water because it's transparent." But this last had left Adele the victim of a *gotcha!*

"This butterfly" (pointing to a drawing) "is called a White Canarian. Its other name is Big White."

"Really! Where did you learn that?"

"Oh, I just made it up."

Conversation closed, the little one flitted off to engage her own reality.

Rory

"Nothing that grieves us can be called little:
by the eternal laws of proportion a child's
loss of a doll and a king's loss of a crown are
events of the same size." —MARK TWAIN

Rory stood stock still, eyes wide, only clutching Mallory's hand a little tighter. There just below his eye level in the dollar store checkout line was a stroller in which reclined a very small baby, perhaps six pounds, gossamer lids stretched over his eyes like the thinnest tissue paper. Rory, though captivated, said nothing. It was only at bedtime, being tucked in to the big hotel bed in protective comfort between his siblings, that he saw fit to broach the subject that had been pressing on his mind. The words came out tentatively, as though he were either sensitive to his mother's sensitivity, aware of treading sacred ground, or embarrassed at his need to ask: "Mama, *was that baby dead?*"

Nadine

"Taking advantage of someone who can't say no should be illegal." —AUTHOR UNKNOWN

Once again the proud owner of a vehicle, thanks to a tinkerer-coworker who fixed them up as a hobby, Gage found himself drifting on a regular basis through the old neighborhood. Avoiding a route that would take him into eye contact with Lauren's childhood home—it was the potential for eye contact in the opposite direction that worried him—he took to frequenting the shaded semicircular lane that skirted the park on the other side. As he knew would be the case, more often than not between the hours of one and two (his belated lunch hour) Nadine would be at her perch on the green bench, as erect and absorbed as a dog taking in the barrage of sensory stimuli from a car window. If Aunt Nadine was anything it was dependable—unpredictable in her quirky way but still utterly reliable when it came to the big things. At whatever level her mind functioned—something not even "Mom" really understood—she was engaged with life on her terms and satisfied.

Adele kept an eye on that bench, Gage knew; she could see it from the picture window. But she couldn't see further into the park; her vision was cut off by the high fence of the homeowner whose property adjoined it.

The day came when Gage parked alongside the crescent road and ambled in the direction of the bench, sack lunch in hand, nonchalantly testing the waters. Aunt Nadine, without appearing to focus on him (she reminded him of one of those disconcerting oil portraits in which you can't tell which way the eyes are looking), knew him immediately despite two-and-a-half intervening years without contact. To her the break had been immaterial; she didn't appear surprised to see him as much as delighted. Squealing, she enthusiastically patted the seat beside her. Gage chose instead to lean companionably against a tree a few feet removed.

Nadine could understand, Gage knew that well enough; her intellectual ability was much higher than her manner suggested. And she could keep a secret. Not feeling the need to share her inner self with other human beings, she would relish an idea or plan, satisfied to mull it over gleefully in her mind. Still, to be on the safe side, Gage would reacquaint slowly enough to make certain of her trust.

Lauren

"The notion by [many] women that every man that comes into their lives want[s] something from them is overrated; some come to fulfill and restore." —POB BISMARK

Lauren, playing it cool to avoid drawing Adele's attention to her date, breezed out of the house at around seven, casually announcing her intention to meet a classmate over a cup of coffee (girlfriend was the implication, she hoped). Lannie was out of school, meaning that there was no homework, and the family seemed settled for the evening with no undo load on Adele. Hugs and kisses with the usual reminder to "be good for Nanna" preceded her departure.

If Adele felt a twinge of resentment over her youngest daughter's readiness to leave three children in her care, she didn't let on; from previous conversations Lauren knew this to be something of an issue and had already determined to do more with the kids during the summer months. Adele's own feelings were mixed, but the prospect of some social life for her daughter seemed fair and reasonable. Lauren, though at times slightly too eager to capitulate her single-parent responsibilities based on her mother's availability, was proving herself in many ways to be a good mom, for which Adele was grateful.

Grant was ready and waiting when Lauren arrived, dressed, she noted, with extra care and playing the part of the gentleman she knew him to be. Lauren, relaxed by the unaccustomed circumstances, found it easy to bask in the attention and relaxation. Both were talkative and energized by the other's company. Two hours later Lauren left on her own, making no attempt to stifle her smile.

Jovanny

*"Temptation is the feeling we get when encountered
by an opportunity to do what we innately know
we shouldn't."* —STEVE MARABOLI

Jovanny, by all accounts a good boy, had little to claim as his own. And that day during the final week of kindergarten, when the class was helping Miss Gentry pack up the room for next year, held temptation for him. Assigned to place the small objects from the shelf representing springtime in their box, he found his hand, clutching the plastic bluebird, straying toward his pants pocket. Jovanny would have followed through with pocketing the bauble had not Darius blown the whistle.

Miss Gentry took him aside, wishing with this child in particular that she could forego the responsibility before her, to look the other way and let him cherish the toy. But pointing him in the right direction allowed for no concessions. Jovanny's hang-dog expression and bowed head revealed a shame possibly deeper than she could attribute to the presenting circumstances, but the rule against stealing had to be definite and firmly enforced. There was no question that Jovanny understood the wrongness of his action, and the consequence meted out was standard. But Miss Gentry felt certain after the fact that the heart-to-heart talk between teacher and student overrode the mortification. Jovanny left his teacher's presence, hugged and reassured of her love, with a lesson learned and a memory to cherish.

Grant

*"Concerning all acts of initiative (and creation), there is one
elementary truth that ignorance of which kills countless ideas and
splendid plans: that the moment one definitely commits oneself,
then Providence moves too."* —WILLIAM HUTCHISON MURRAY

For his part, Grant was sure. He'd never before jumped to a conclusion on a first date; his nature was deliberative and his actions carefully thought out. He was hardly calculating, though; far from it, from childhood on he'd been a straight shooter free of ulterior motives. Having secured a second date for the next week, he was contented to take things slowly in deference to her feelings and needs. Lauren had made it clear that, as tempting as it was to include the children on summer outings, she felt it unwise at this juncture to confuse them or raise their hopes. Her oldest, Lannie, had been quite conflicted at four—her age at the time of the split. Though the children's dad was out of the picture, the possibility of hurting any of them had to be avoided.

Grant had never before felt such peace about a relationship or any other major life decision. The Lord, he felt assured, had brought him to the right one—or her to him. Moving forward was up to him.

The one nagging reservation had to do with uncertainty on his part about the depth of her faith commitment and relationship with the Lord. During the Gage years, it was clear, she had taken a long break from church attendance, though she evidently had no adverse feelings on the subject. The children regularly attended services with their nanna, with Lauren accompanying them at least occasionally. If there were to be any rub in the relationship, it would be this: lack of unqualified unity between the two or them in this vital regard would have to be a showstopper.

Adele

*"The more we depend on God the more dependable
we find He is."* —CLIFF RICHARD

"I have seventeen moneys!" Lannie announced airily, opening her purse to display her trove.

"Wow!" Adele responded with an approving smile. "You've been saving."

"No. Momma said okay to take them from her wallet. It was too fat!"

It occurred to Adele that, beyond Lannie's collecting the coins as she would any other "stuff" (collecting is what little girls were all about), they meant little to her. Her security was wholly elsewhere. *Can I say the same about myself?* Adele couldn't help but ask—*all the time?* Her hands alone occupied with folding laundry, the line of thought stayed with her. The second part of the answer, she admitted, had to be no. Living as she did on a fixed income, though she couldn't complain about its adequacy, meant that the bulk of her resources came available on a given date toward the end of each month. The first half of the month, when most of the bills came due, could be problematic. She at times had to hedge and finagle when time and resources put on their joint monthly squeeze. Somehow it all worked, but worry equity seemed necessary to "make it happen."

Back, then, to the first clause: *Can I say the same about myself— that my security is wholly elsewhere?* Adele had already negated the "wholly" (along with "all the time"), but if she took the question without that qualifier she found herself surprised by the answer. Because it seemed to be yes! How easy it was to view herself as coming up short on every self-assessment against the impossible standard of God's law and expectation! Adele wondered whether other believers were hung up in this area, whether, despite God's mandate for his children to be holy, they saw it as presumptuous to acknowledge the Spirit's enabling them to actually get some things right! This was getting convoluted, but the conclusion she seemed to be approaching felt important.

The truth was that Adele found it difficult to imagine *not* being secure in God, her strength. In some sense that dependency was so basic that it defined her. Granted, her security in her status (finances included) and her satisfaction with her income were two different matters, not always in synch. But dwelling on the positive side of that comparison, what a comfort to *know* that her needs would always be met! How different—how unbelievably difficult—life would be without that assurance! And yet so many lacked it . . .

Luke

"Intentional living is the art of making our own choices
before others' choices make us." —RICHIE NORTON

Observing Luke's toddler swimming lesson, Adele chuckled as a trio of two and three year olds experienced their first pool encounters. One by one the initiates were to jump from the side of the pool into the instructor's waiting arms. The little boy up front, before Luke, made a few false starts. The intentionality was there: he bobbed, he stooped, he tensed, he inclined forward. But his feet stayed firmly planted on the tile.

Intentionality alone, Adele chuckled, doesn't get us where we need to be. Thinking back to Jesus' well-known words "The spirit is willing, but the flesh is weak," she wondered whether it was the boy's spirit or his limbs that were momentarily paralyzed.

Gage

"When a man is in despair, it means that he still
believes in something." —DMITRI SHOSTAKOVICH

The night Gage fell off the wagon wasn't a complete surrender; some inner restraint seemed to be operative, pulling him back even in his drunken state. But it was Mallory's imploring gaze after he had stumbled back into the hotel room that made all the difference. No, he wouldn't plunge into a backward free fall this time—not now, after what he'd done to her and in light of what he owed her. Not now, he realized with a start, that he had come to love this new family.

Lexie

"It was nice growing up with someone like you—someone to lean on,
someone to count on—someone to tell on!" —AUTHOR UNKNOWN

Lexie, Adele overheard, was explaining to Luke the vagaries of birth order: "You're the littlest, Lannie's the oldest, and I'm the middlest." But he was having none of it. Clearly affronted, he objected with flashing eyes: "I *not* little! I big boy. Nanna said."

Lannie, taking on the peacemaker role that came as her birthright, explained the situation in slightly altered terms, assuring Luke, "You're the biggest *brother* in the house. Lexie's a little bigger, but she's a sister."

Asserting the power of his station, Luke stretched himself to full height. And finding nothing objectionable in the logic, Lexie accepted her own status. Sister in the middle, surrounded by strength, suited her just fine; it sounded like a sheltered place to be.

Mallory

"Extreme poverty is not only a condition
of unsatisfied material needs. It is often accompanied
by a degrading state of powerlessness." —PETER SINGER

The novelty of the hotel room's TV after the stay in North Carolina was beginning to wear off for her offspring as Mallory was emerging from her lengthy checkout. It occurred to her with something of a start that the kids needed toys. The hotel parking lot was no place to run, and the place's reputation as a halfway house for parolees (it seemed as though a quarter of the occupants, both men and women, at any given time sported ankle tethers), made for a dicey situation, with the space between the four walls affording a prison-like haven for children chafing for action.

The McDonald's Playplace within easy walking distance was a Godsend—a playground with its own four walls affording security to a grieving mom afflicted with an overactive imagination when it came to her surviving children. As long as she made a purchase of some sort, even if only small fries all around, no one questioned her presence at a table for an extended period.

The Saturday after her monthly government subsidy hit her card, Mallory splurged on Happy Meals. The drawing card this time around was as much the toy as the unvarying nutritional fare. So the casual announcement from the girl behind the counter ("Sorry, we're all out of boy toys") took her aback; no doubt stated factually, it struck her as dismissive and insensitive.

Mallory accepted the three meals, Daisy's delight in the Barbie ballerina figure registering in the back of her mind as she observed the disappointment in the other two upturned faces. The boys, little troopers from a combination of experience and compliant natures, accepted the news well enough, contenting themselves with playing and eating, pretty much in that order.

It was only as they made their way toward the door an hour or so later that the mother relented, pushing aside her pride. Sidling up to the far edge of the counter at the first lull, she requested in her most dignified voice two more Barbie figures, which she handed off, one at a time, to her eager sons.

Daisy

*"Without leaps of imagination or dreaming,
we lose the excitement of possibilities. Dreaming, after
all, is a form of planning."* —GLORIA STEINEM

Though the situation was explained to Daisy in positive, child-friendly terms, the little girl was embarrassed by the prospect of having to repeat the first grade. She had failed, she knew, yet what she could have done differently eluded her. The same child who a few short months earlier had attempted on her own to organize a household in North Carolina now faced the recognition that she was too dumb to read or do math. Try as she might, her efforts were thwarted by those figures on the page that seemed so treacherously to dance and tumble about, mocking her attempts to pin them down. Concentration too was a problem: her mind had a habit of somersaulting to unrelated issues. Daisy recognized herself to be shamefully deficient in some fundamental way.

Mrs. Trumball, suspecting the trouble, took her aside one morning while the children worked silently at their desks. Her arm around the stiff, humiliated figure, the teacher explained how very fortunate she was to be able to continue Daisy's acquaintance for another year. Missing two months of school would be hard for any little girl, but the way Daisy had come back and kept trying had impressed her very much. Next year Daisy would be older and even more grown up. She was already smart, but she would have a chance to be a leader in September when school started again. Daisy knew so much about how first grade worked that Mrs. Trumball had it in mind that she could be a great helper.

Carefully broaching the subject of a difficult year for Daisy, Mrs. Trumball predicted that things were going to turn around—that next year would be *way better*. Mrs. Trumball wasn't sure what she had said that might have made a difference, but it was apparent she had touched a chord. Daisy flicked up her gaze briefly to meet her teacher's before throwing her arms around her. Unaccustomed to the prospect of something to look forward to, Daisy began to will herself to move beyond this year.

Adele's Devotion: A June Reading

ECLIPSE

**"He has rescued us from the dominion
of darkness and brought us into the kingdom
of the Son he loves." (COLOSSIANS 1:13)**

*Both the dark domain and the kingdom of light perme-
ate the New Testament and our world, the one seeking
to promote and the other to expel the blackness of sin and
its consequences. Their interplay is seen and felt continu-
ously, each seeking to impinge upon the other with stabbing
point and counterpoint.*

*We as Christians, though, too often fail to recognize
the mismatch between the two in terms of power and per-
manence. If we would only be bolder to claim and acclaim
the superiority of our side, we would sense the darkness*

beating a hasty retreat. I like this analogy from Beverly Sills: "Christians should never fail to sense the operation of an angelic glory. It forever eclipses the world of demonic powers, as the sun does a candle's light."

July

Gage

"We can easily forgive a child who is afraid of the dark; the real tragedy of life is when men are afraid of the light." —PLATO

Gage's approach to his coworker was a study in nonchalance. "Hey, I was telling you about this friend of mine, the one who did the three terms of Desert Shield? This PTSD thing's hitting him hard. He wants to work, but what can you do when you're so shot you can't sleep?"

"If I were him, I'd take something. I'm no doctor, but I swear by this halcion. Stuff hits fast and hard—out like a light long enough to totally zonk, and then it's over. Side effects can be nasty, I've heard, but I haven't had a problem. Tell you what, rather than have him go through the hassle of getting a script before he knows his tolerance—it's a controlled substance, you know—why don't I bring one in to let him try?"

"Thanks! Better two, if you can spare 'em. A couple of nights should give 'em a fair go."

"You got it. I'll have 'em tomorrow. He's gonna thank you!"

Jovanny

"Children's games are hardly games. Children are never more serious than when they play." —MONTAIGNE

"What're you boys doing?" Mallory's voice from the bed was peevish. She was fighting a sick headache, forehead and eyes covered by a wet washcloth. The air conditioner was running, but ineffectively so; the television was blaring afternoon soaps; and all three children, cooped up in the tiny room with the shades drawn against the heat and glare, felt stir-crazy and acted so. Jovanny was weaving his way around the room with clumping steps and exaggeratedly uncoordinated gestures. Rory, delighted with the new game, was right at his heels, copycatting some movements and ad-libbing others.

Daisy, unamused and glaring, filled in the obvious for her mother's enlightenment, her voice constricted: "Can't you tell, Mama? They're *drunk!*"

Lauren

"Eternity has a way of letting us all grow up." —SHANNON L. ALDER

Lauren's two sisters and two brothers all lived within hours of Adele's home, and members of the larger family got together several times each year. All four of Lauren's older siblings, along with at least some of their family members (most of the older children were no longer readily available for family trips), had made their way to Adele's home for a celebration of the fourth. Lauren's two sisters, whose husbands and children had returned immediately to home and jobs, had each arranged for additional time off and had stayed on at the hotel for an extra couple of days before driving home together. Lauren was to meet them today over an extended lunch hour.

Denise and Janelle, aged forty-two and forty, respectively, had mixed feelings about their younger sister's relationship, not based on any apparent problem—Grant sounded too good to be true!—but simply because their "little" sister and her children had already been hurt, and their protective instincts were kicking in. Knowing she had been impetuous in the past, they wanted to verify that all signs were positive.

Aware from their mother that Grant was a Christian who took his faith seriously, the sisters also felt a responsibility to make sure Lauren understood the importance to the probable union of mutual spiritual sincerity. Grant, who had never been married, needed to understand where she was coming from and what he was getting into, very much including the fatherhood and family and spiritual headship roles he was poised to adopt.

The lunch came off without a hitch; the three sisters were refreshed by each other's company, with Denise and Janelle impressed with Lauren's openness and obvious maturation. The three had never before melded quite like this, on equal terms for the first time in Lauren's adulthood.

Rory

"Closed in a room, my imagination becomes the universe,
and the rest of the world is missing out." —CRISS JAMI

If Rory had experienced doubt—and he had—it was only seldom in himself. That very certainty, or the absence of any reason to question it, had seen him through two plus difficult opening years. He was in the midst of that sky's-the-limit age during which even the sky posed no boundary for his imagination. A hotel bath towel would have made a fine cape, but equally fine and more readily accessible was the one flapping behind from his imagination. The tiny room with its walls and ceiling hadn't yet affected its scope; Rory was small, the ceiling was high, and so was his reach, if not physically then mentally, emotionally, and even spiritually— though on that last score he had little frame of reference. Boredom had yet to enter either his vocabulary or his awareness, and his experience was inadequate for comparisons. Blessedly, Rory's cocoon of naiveté still provided a secure place within which to develop.

Lannie

"I am glad I will not be young in a future
without wilderness." —ALDO LEOPOLD

Lannie's firm stance on environmental issues pointed in both Lauren's and Adele's minds to some effective teaching efforts associated with her first-grade instruction. "See. My washcloth is still wet," she announced to Lauren one July evening. "That's why I don't squeeze it out. It saves the environment." Lauren, observing the slow drip of the wadded cloth onto the floor, didn't follow the logical progression of that argument, but that her daughter's environmental sensitivities were intact she had no doubt.

A few nights later, seated with the gathered family on the veranda between 9:00 and 10:00 p.m. (the kids holding jars in preparation for catching fireflies), the child commented on the delayed onset of darkness: "God is wasting power." Adele pointed out that the "free" light from God—light, as part of him, as *who he is*, costs him nothing—allows us to save on electricity used for illumination.

Still, exercising her childish prerogative to have it both ways, Lannie's perceptions of creature comforts based on energy consumption tended in opposing directions. A day or so later, coming in from a bike ride in the heat to the air conditioning, she flopped onto the couch, ran a hand across her perspiring forehead, and enthused, "This makes me feel even younger!"

Arabelle

"To sit with a dog on a hillside on a glorious afternoon is to be back in Eden, where doing nothing was not boring—it was peace." —MILAN KUNDERA

"Walking" Lauren's nearly full-grown lab-mix pup in the heat of the day was an exercise in patience. Arabelle, who could lurch Adele along with bursts of exuberance when it was cool, would become an avid sunbather at midday in July. She'd meander along for a short while, sniffing the ground with full-body engagement, after which she'd plop down on the sidewalk or grass, nest her head on her paws, and look up at Adele with soulful eyes. At times she'd roll over until Adele consented to scratch her belly, but it seemed as though she could lie there, contented, for the duration.

This morning, overheated and impatient at the prospect of an open-ended duration, Adele broke into a slow fume. Mr. Rubingh called out from his porch rocker, "That dog's a mule, isn't she?"

Lexie

"I can't get to sleep, Nanna."
"Just go back to bed and find another position."
"It's the only position I have."

Lexie, Adele couldn't help but notice, was developing a fixation with death. Lauren, who insisted on the euphemism "passed on" for the children's usage, was on the other hand less than a stickler about the detective programs she permitted herself to watch in their presence—or proximity, as she preferred to view it. Lauren was convinced the kids paid no attention.

Adele suspected the real reason had to do with Lauren's felt need for some entertainment downtime after a day's work but tried not to interfere too much. She had to admit a preference, though, for those structured evenings when Lauren was in class or out with Grant.

One evening in July, Lexie approached Adele with a solemn statement that took her totally aback. She edged up, head bowed, and spoke in a whisper that trailed off into a whimper: "Nanna, when I die you'll have to stay in the house while I fight the bad people." Mystified at first, Adele realized with a start that Lexie equated death with murder and felt the need to shelter her nanna when this inevitable fate confronted her—Lexie herself. Adele hoped her attempts at explanation and assurance would make the difference.

A few nights later the narrator of a documentary Adele was viewing commented that the life of the individual being featured had "fallen apart" following a setback. "What does that mean?" Lexie asked, alarmed. Adele explained in simple terms, going on to note that the life of a Christian need never fall apart, and why. "But what about if their nanna passes on?" Lexie pressed in real concern. She had evidently thought this one through. In a wave of conviction Adele realized the danger of careless exposure of the little ones to possibilities beyond imagining.

Grant

"Guidance means I can count on God. Commitment means God can count on me." —ANONYMOUS

Lauren wasn't proud of her years of laxness in the exercise of her faith, though she had tended to view the issue as a bad habit she could break on the basis of willpower at any time she chose. The slackness had started shortly after she and Gage had launched out on their own and come to realize that they could get away with relaxing a standard that—though less than a rule—had for all her life been a given. At first simply sleeping in and enjoying a leisurely breakfast and perhaps a walk (they'd chosen those first few weeks to view this as an alternate form of Sabbath resting) had come as a welcome change of pace.

Over those early years the routine had morphed into doing something special together, even—and perhaps especially—if little or no financial outlay was involved. By the time Lannie had entered the picture, though, a combination of stress, apathy, and guilt would have kept the couple away from the Lord's house even if they'd consciously considered a day of resting in him as an option.

In her present situation Lauren was grateful for Adele's regular church attendance with and, more importantly, her faithful spiritual nurture of the children. As their mother she never expressed negativity on the subject and lived a clean—in her mind even an exemplary—life, going so far as to attend worship services periodically with the family. Knowing that the onus for the children's faith development rested squarely on Adele's back, though, was convenient and comfortable.

The problem was that neither Lauren nor Gage—whose experience had been that of following his girlfriend as the unspoken spiritual leader—had ever made a faith commitment. Both had liked church and felt comfortable with all things God; as willing hangers on they'd followed along the path demonstrated by Roddy and Adele. Lauren, always the couple's free spirit, had differed from her brothers and sisters in some basic regards since early childhood; her independent streak, which had applied about equally in those younger years to her parents and the divine, had been masked by the lack of a rebellious attitude to call attention to it. Lauren had acquiesced with a sweet spirit but without commitment or a recognition of its lack.

Lannie's expressed concern about Lauren's habits had begun to rankle, but so far Lauren had managed to shuck Jiminy Cricket from her shoulder. Now Grant's wholly different outlook on the importance of worship and Christian service convicted her to the point that she determined she would at some appropriate point in their relationship resume her long-neglected routine. Adele, Grant knew, couldn't be more thrilled, but he needed more from Lauren than a concession if the relationship were to progress. The issue was nonnegotiable; anything less than wholehearted dedication on her part would still mean cutting things off.

The couple discussed the matter at length, and through Grant's gentle prodding Lauren began to understand that her belief, though intact to the degree it had ever been, was not only inadequate but was being systematically undermined by neglect. His insistence on a joint faith commitment for a godly marriage— something Roddy and Adele had taken for granted their youngest understood—set her to thinking in unaccustomed ways. In the end some counseling with a pastor colleague of Grant's dad ("premarital" in Grant's mind only if the hurdle could be resolved) made the difference.

The change in Lauren was genuine—in no way coerced by the corner into which she might have felt herself backed—as evidenced by a clear change in her manner and outlook. It can be dicey, Grant recognized, to identify the fruit of Spirit intervention in an already giving personality, but neither he nor Adele entertained any doubt that a transformed Lauren had emerged.

Luke

"Children are unpredictable. You never know what inconsistency they're going to catch you in next." —FRANKLIN P. JONES

"Nanna, you said don't means don't."

"That's right, Luker. How come?"

"You said no singing if Lexie doesn't like it."

"I did?"

"Uh huh. How come you're singing?"

"Oops. Let's see if Lexie likes it now. Lexie, is it okay if Luke sings?"

"Yup. *Jesus Loves Me.*"

"Jesus loves me . . ."

"Keep going."

"I can't. The words are all gone."

"Well, try it again and we'll help you."

"*Je*—help me!"

Luke, connoisseur of "funny jokes," found himself to be hilarious but forgot about the singing. Moments later Adele softly picked up the tune that had been running through her head.

Daisy

*"Forgetting isn't the key to moving on.
Remembering is, because only once we've
remembered can we forget."* —EMMA HART

Ironically, though Daisy had pledged after the conversation with Mrs. Trumball to forget those recent pivotal events that seemed to define her life, it was with time becoming imperative not only to remember but to keep the memories tangible. Dealing with them in the first place and then keeping them intact seemed necessary to their survival, and thus to their reality, a task she took upon herself with quiet determination. This was altogether opposite the continuing choice her mama was making, only to find herself haunted by the remembrances that wouldn't be squelched.

Daisy's intuitive response, though a secondary one, would prove the wiser.

A new box of 64 crayons and a spiral book of wide-ruled writing paper, gifts from Gage, had called up in her an explosion of remembering. Page after page of yellow-haired babies in different poses had flown from her fingers, a memory book of sorts in the absence of photos—even though the "memories," beyond the first, with the swaddled bath towel, were pure speculation.

Her brothers present but asleep and Mallory sitting idle on the occasional chair, Daisy saw her opportunity.

Mallory

*"Simply touching a difficult memory with some
slight willingness to heal begins to soften the holding
and tension around it."* —STEPHEN LEVINE

"I remember her." Daisy's whispered words to Mama came tentative in the privacy of the room otherwise occupied by the sleeping boys, startling Mallory only slightly. With an effort she allowed her mind to ease around them, incorporating them; to her surprise she liked the sensation.

"You do? What was she like?"

"Like you!"

"Really? How?"

"All beautiful and yellow with soft cheeks. Not like me."

"Your cheeks *are* soft!" (caressing one of them lightly, like a butterfly kiss barely making contact).

"I'm all brown. Not beige."

"When I was a little girl one of my crayons was called flesh. They don't use that name anymore."

"Why not?"

"Because flesh—skin—comes in all different colors—all wonderful!"

"I love you, Mama!"

"And I love *you, my beautiful girl!*"

Adele

"'After all,' Anne had said to Marilla once, 'I believe the
nicest and sweetest days are not those on which anything very
splendid or wonderful or exciting happens but just those that
bring simple little pleasures, following one another softly,
like pearls slipping off a string.'" —L. M. MONTGOMERY

Adele loved little better than the twitter of birds heralding the early dawn before the children rose. Her bedroom faced the backyard to the west, and the stillness of that time could be almost palpable. When the birds began singing the sound seemed to come from every direction. Perhaps part of what made that chorus so special was that it had no competition. She listened, yes, but felt herself to be as fully aware of the prevailing stillness as of the song that punctuated it.

An upside of summer vacation was Adele's ability to forego setting the alarm. She would listen with half an ear as Lauren readied herself for her early shift and then doze again until the children's circadian rhythms kicked in, alerting them almost simultaneously that the sun was already "up." They would pad into Adele's room like clockwork between 7:10 and 7:15, after which they'd establish themselves in the living room for some unstructured time while their nanna, mostly awake, dozed unnecessarily until 8:00 (Nadine tended to be a late riser).

Adele often found that forty-five-minute period to be the highlight of her day, an opportunity to reflect and plan and ponder. No, it wasn't a deliberate prayer time, though she sensed subliminal dialogue going on. Still, these minutes for Adele were sacramental. What a blessing to begin each day alert but unalarmed!

Nadine

"I never, even for a moment, doubted what they'd told me.
This is why it is that adults . . . can, unwittingly, be

cruel: they cannot imagine doubt's complete absence.
They have forgotten." —DAVID FOSTER WALLACE

August 1—tomorrow—a Friday this year, and Gage's day off, was to be a big day for Nadine, though she didn't yet know it. Gage's lunch hours in the park had become routine, and Nadine expected him. He'd given her no hint of his best-laid plan, but today two crushed halcion 0.125 tablets occupied a baggie within his brown bag. Gage felt uncomfortably like a dealer approaching a client.

The plan had to be simple, but he gave Nadine credit for more than she let on. Everything banked on her coming through, but somehow he had little doubt. Nadine liked surprises, had no moral scruples, and would be flattered by his trust. Though sitting next to her on the bench would afford him optimal ability to prepare her for follow-through, he wasn't about to take that risk the day before the visit. He devoted ample time to the task, taking it slowly, until he felt satisfied she understood and was on board.

Nadine cackled like a delighted schoolgirl sharing a secret behind the teacher's back, hand over mouth to stifle any sound. The magic was for Adele—only her!—and she couldn't know about it beforehand. Nadine was to take the kids to the park when the magic hit, so her sister could enjoy the spell all on her own, asleep. Iced tea, that was the ticket. She'd just pop the magic in, and that tea would taste so sweet. *Don't tell! Don't tell!*

Adele's Devotion: A July Reading

WHERE THERE'S LIFE . . .

"He has blinded their eyes and hardened their hearts,
so they can neither see with their eyes, nor understand with
their hearts, nor turn—and I would heal them." (JOHN 12:40)

Blaise Pascal observed that "In faith there is enough light
for those who want to believe and enough shadows to blind

those who don't." John's quote from Isaiah 6:10, above, comes not from Jesus' mouth but from the Father's, as part of Isaiah's commission. What sounds like prescriptive language there is actually descriptive. God doesn't want anyone to reject his Son but recognizes that many will.

Who of us doesn't have within our circle of concern at least one individual whose disinterest in the things of God hurts our hearts? It can help to bear in mind that it's never our place to write off another person. God doesn't give up easily. Listen again to the pathos in his closing words: "—and I would heal them."

August

Nadine

"For people with autism, the details jump straight out at us first of all, and then only gradually, detail by detail, does the whole image float up into focus." —NAOKI HIGASHIDA

She could keep a secret, though she couldn't recall ever before having been entrusted with one. Lunch on the veranda—that was the routine for a summer day, usually rain or shine; Adele didn't like for Nadine's sake to vary the rhythm too much. Today was shine, a garish mid-eighties at almost noon. All five, the two women and three kids, were settled with plates on laps—the little ones sharing the top step, facing the yard. Arabelle, increasingly trustworthy, had plopped at the women's feet, slightly tilted head resting on paws, a question mark in her upturned eyes.

Iced tea, unsweetened, was the drink of choice for the older sisters, and today was no exception. It wasn't often Nadine expressed an opinion, but this morning she surprised Adele by requesting more ice. Adele rose dutifully, accepted the glass, and disappeared back into the kitchen. Nadine lost no time; she'd been clutching the folded baggie tightly in her palm and now dropped its contents into the remaining glass of tea before depositing it back into her pocket. Gage had said stir, and stir she did, using the spoon for her fruit cocktail.

Adele reemerged almost immediately, Nadine accepting the doubly-iced tea with a 100-watt smile. *At least she appreciates it,* Adele acknowledged, making a mental note to add the extra ice beforehand the next time around. The lunchtime routine included the better part of an hour on the porch, after which Nadine would disappear down the block, bound for the green bench. The kids, either scarfing their lunches or losing interest before they were finished, were soon off playing in the front yard. The homemaker typically used this downtime to sip her tea, enjoy the fresh air, and even at times fit in the day's devotional reading.

She drank a little faster than usual today in the heat and considered going in for a partial refill. Feeling unaccountably sleepy, though, Adele indulged herself instead with the luxury of a few minutes of shuteye. No one would object, and she was good at keeping her ears open while relaxing . . .

Aware by the depths of her sister's breathing and by her brief snort that she was fully out, absorbed in her magic dream, Nadine rose and made her way down the stairs, beckoning the children to follow her down the sidewalk. Luke and Arabelle were game enough, but Lexie, and to a much greater extent Lannie, had to be convinced. "Leave her 'lone," directed Aunt Nadine in a tone that left no room for argument. "She's tired, see?" The clot of children, with their dog, followed their unlikely pied piper down the street in the shimmering sun, in the order in which they'd been persuaded. Lannie, concerned about Nanna's exhaustion but agreeing to afford her the needed space, followed reluctantly and with backward glances.

Luke

"Accidents ambush the unsuspecting, often violently, just like love." —ANDREW DAVIDSON

Gage always came from the wiggle road, nearer the small lake— more a glorified pond, really. Nadine, anticipating the children's surprise, along with his approval of her pulling off her assignment, walked this morning with a wide grin, her maniacal gaze on high beam. Not immediately seeing the old car, she acquiesced to Luke's request for Hidenseek. There weren't many trees and otherwise only a few picnic tables and a trashcan or two within easy running distance. But Luke noticed something else: the murky water had a greenish cast, and he couldn't see far down. Besides which the cool waters looked inviting under the midday sun. Luker had spotted an ideal—not to mention *big*— place of concealment!

Lannie being "it" for the first round (she was proud of her ability to count all the way to one hundred), squinched her eyes tightly shut, pressed her forehead against a tree trunk, and began to count slowly and loudly to give the hiders plenty of time. Lexie scuttled off in the direction of a trashcan, while Luke bolted toward the inviting water. Aunt Nadine, who had never gotten the hang of hiding—or seeking—would likely function as a cheerleader, clapping and whooping as the action unfolded.

Luke's entrance into the ideal hiding place was confident (his teacher had always caught him earlier in the summer in his swimming lessons) and immediate; he hurtled headfirst and spread-eagled, like a parachutist from a plane, gleeful over his plan. Aunt Nadine splashed in directly behind him in her socks and tennies, yelling *"Here I am!"* while helping hold his head under water. Arabelle, seeing her best friend in danger, yelped piteously before running off full tilt for a different brand of help.

Lannie

"The question is not what you look at,
but what you see." —HENRY DAVID THOREAU

Lannie, slower on the draw due to her counting, turned in time to see the dog's headlong barrel. Farther from the lake than Lexie, she spotted frantic activity at its bank. A man—Was it *Daddy??*—was scrabbling with Aunt Nadine, finally prizing her hands from something in the water and pushing her roughly toward shore. The man himself tumbled into the shallow water, emerging with an apparently sleeping, and dripping, Luke. The man—yes, it *was* Daddy—was *hurting* her sleeping brother, pushing him in the chest!—no, he was bending over, close up to his mouth now.

Lannie had seen enough to know that Luke was in trouble. Maybe Aunt Nadine too. Knowing precisely where to go for help (despite the risk of disturbing a nap), she went the way of Arabelle, slower but fully as determined, blubbering as hard as the lab was yowling.

Adele

"We have to be braver than we think we can be,
because God is constantly calling us to be more
than we are." —MADELEINE L'ENGLE

Adele startled at Arabelle's hectic approach. The dog was barking frenetically, in a sharp, pitched yip that screamed SOS as surely as a chorus of sirens. Despite a lightheaded, sluggish feeling, Adele awoke readily enough. *What had hit her? What was going on?* The dog's frenzy signified much more than the presence of a squirrel! And where was everybody? As though on cue, her eye caught sight of a frantic Lannie, tripping toward her, unaccompanied, on the sidewalk, nearly blinded by tears.

Adele needed no explanation before reacting; making no attempt to collect her scattered thoughts, she nearly stumbled down the steps, pushing, *pushing* against her fuzziness in the direction of the deserted green bench. As though for dramatic effect the sirens kicked in at that moment, coming from all directions, it seemed. Lannie collided with her nanna before nearly collapsing into her arms, huffing barely coherent exclamations that sounded like "Luke," "Daddy," and "Nadine." Barely slowing to steer her around, Adele clung to her granddaughter, in part for support and in part to propel the little girl without losing her own staggering momentum.

Lexie

"That's not my dad at all, that's just some stranger
hanging around in my memory." —JAROD KINTZ

Fifteen minutes later Lexie stood silent, slightly behind her great-aunt and sister, pallid and gaping. She'd had no idea water could put someone to sleep like Luke was. Or that it could get into your nozzelers (maybe your other head holes too!) or spurt out from your mouth like a hose turning on and off.

Perplexed, she had recognized immediately the man with the candy from preschool. *Why was he here now?* But there was another, deeper stirring the little one couldn't identify. Lannie, as though reading the question, filled her in: "He's our daddy. Remember?" Reassuringly, she grasped her sister's hand. "He helped Luke." Both girls, though confused and frightened, were duly impressed that their long-absent daddy had found them just when Luker needed him.

Gage

"Does anything in nature despair except man?
An animal with a foot caught in a trap
does not seem to despair. It is too busy trying
to survive." —MAY SARTON

Gage, distraught, had immediately relinquished his attempts at CPR to the paramedics. Now, standing helpless at just enough distance to allow the professionals to work (it was impossible from this vantage to determine whether the boy breathed), he gave in to the agony of coherent thought.

Everything, *everything* was his fault; he didn't need to be told that. But he'd "met" and "known" this baby for a shorter time even than his angel sister. This one couldn't stop breathing! "God, help him breathe!! *Don't let my baby die!*" As Gage resigned himself to torment he dropped to his knees, head in hands, blubbering like a child in ragged, shuddering sobs.

Gage was only partially aware of being gathered into a maternal embrace, to which he relinquished himself wholly. Adele would sort out the facts at a more opportune moment. Nadine and the little girls, subdued and wide-eyed, huddled close by. For the moment this one, broken and anguished, needed her most.

Lauren

"'Good works is giving to the poor and the helpless, but divine works is showing them their worth to the One who matters.'" —CRISS JAMI

This was the way Lauren found them when a short time later she arrived on the scene, escorted by a coworker. Luke, unresponsive, was ready to be moved to the waiting ambulance, so she had little time to react to the shock of Gage's unexplained presence or obvious brokenness.

At eight o'clock that evening, sitting at the hospital crib of her inert son, his motionless hand in her own, a benumbed Lauren tried to make sense of the afternoon. Luke was ashen, though the tinges of blue had receded from around his lips. His eyelids, closed, fluttered periodically, and little twinges suggested to her that he might be reliving the experience; the possibility of seizure activity she expunged from her consciousness. Luker breathed on his own, though assisted by oxygen. The prognosis was guardedly positive; the doctor warned that a degree of brain damage might or might not be immediately detectable.

In terms of what had happened and why, the story that had unfolded so far, based on information provided by Gage himself, the police, the paramedics, Adele, the little girls, and even Aunt Nadine and Gage's coworker who had supplied the halcion tablets, seemed bizarre almost beyond belief. A remorseful Gage, upon his arrest hours earlier, had freely admitted his arrangement of the whole affair; he had gone so far as to voluntarily tie in the January incident at Lexie's preschool but had insisted throughout his confession that his intention had never been anything beyond seeing and speaking with his children.

Gage's boss had posted bail. Extensive investigation would, of course, follow; the uncertain medical outcome for Luke left unanswerable question marks at this moment. One way or another, Gage's cooperation would do a great deal toward moving the case along to his sentencing sometime in the fall. Possible charges could include attempted kidnapping, violation of the personal protection order against the children, and battery in conjunction with Adele's drugging. (Mother and daughter had learned to their surprise that, though Adele could opt for a civil suit if she felt she had a case, this last issue depended not on her decision whether or not to press charges but on the district attorney's determination of whether Gage's action toward her had constituted a crime.)

Lauren, a subdued Grant at her side, had time to reflect on her feelings for Gage. She felt neither hostility nor pity for her husband of nine years, nor did she love him. But she was finding to her surprise that, despite the entire episode being Gage's fault, she grudgingly respected him for rescuing their son.

At that moment Gage and Mallory appeared in the doorway—Gage still utterly contrite and Mallory the picture of dis-ease. (His appearance here was not a violation of the PPO, which did not prohibit contact in a public, protected setting.) Both women registered a reaction as they recognized one another as that other mom whose life had so briefly touched her own at McDonalds more than seven months earlier. Grant, quickly assessing the situation, rose immediately to offer his chair to Mallory before striding over to Gage, arm outstretched for a handshake.

This unexpected gesture appeared to overwhelm Gage. Having heard nothing of Lauren's dating—*Why hadn't he considered that a possibility, or even a probability?*—he was thrown off by the presence of the other man. But it was the kindness, something he'd been sure he could never again hope for from anyone, that unstrung him. Gage did indeed reach out his hand, but it was through a gush of tears, to stabilize himself from crumpling onto the floor or even into Grant's arms.

Grant, master of the situation, did indeed enfold the man, helping him to the chair by the bedside that Lauren had immediately vacated. Gage hunched there next to Mallory, rocking and bent nearly double, head in hands and making a keening sound none of the others could recall having heard before. Both of the women—the two women in the world who knew Gage intimately—were stunned to the point of inaction, other than Mallory standing abruptly and seeking refuge, or retreat, next to Lauren, who embraced her. Sensing Gage's guilt and feeling unaccountably an accomplice, Mallory too burst into tears—utterly silent, wracking sobs that emerged from the deepest chasm of despair. The four adults remained in these poses—Gage on the chair supported by a kneeling Grant with the women standing behind, Adele attending to Mallory. This is the way Adele, in her turn, found them.

Mallory

"Childhood should be carefree, playing in the sun; not living a nightmare in the darkness of the soul." —DAVE PELZER

Until Gage, Mallory had never in her lifetime experienced a semblance of real love. She knew love, all right, from her own side—a fierce, mama bear attachment to her offspring and, more recently, the surprise of intense feeling for Gage. It had begun from both sides as infatuation—the only connection she had known to any man; love was a sensation she lacked the experience to identify, let alone quantify. They'd been through a great deal together in a short time, she and Gage, and she was grateful for his sticking with her through the ugly and unbearable; it had taken some time for her to acknowledge or even recognize the extent to which he, too, grieved.

Mallory had been nothing more to either of her other children's fathers than a "baby mama," and even at that each of the infants had been immediately perceived as a liability and a killjoy—unwanted baggage for which both fathers seemed to view her as culpable, not to mention a responsibility neither had any intention of hefting. The pregnancies themselves had turned them off; Alejandro had hung in there for two, though Jahmeel had been off running soon after morning sickness had dialed down her drive.

Looking back further, something she didn't care to do, there had been only incest and abuse from a variety of men, including her own father—her mother knowledgeable (even complicit?) but choosing to look the other way. Mallory's mother had objected to having a girl in the first place—her unfortunate gender Mallory had construed from as far back as she could remember as her fault too. One way or another, her mother had systematically punished her for who she was. The little girl had been flanked by brothers, older and younger, both of whom had experienced their growing up years, as far as she could see, as little kings. She had a vague recollection of being penetrated by the older but had so blocked her girlhood memories that she no longer trusted her recall.

Mallory was determined to do better by Daisy—and would have done so for Gage's daughter too—had she had the opportunity to do more than attempt to nurse her once before falling into a stupored sleep in that dank house. Now Gage, the first person she'd ever come close to trusting, had done something underhanded, something unspeakable that involved his own children, something evidently premeditated to which he had never alluded in her presence—most of the details of which she had as yet to discover and sort out.

Accustomed to shame, she was prepared to accept it unquestioningly through association, though she had no clear idea from Gage's distress what had actually occurred. Despite her tears, Mallory's gaze darted toward the crib to take in the motionless little boy who had so moved her at McDonalds by his instant, hand-in-hand friendship with Rory. *Gage's son??* That in itself was too much to fathom. *And Gage's fault that he, who should be running and laughing, lay unconscious and perhaps fighting for life in the crib? The son of the very Gage who seemed so taken with Daisy, Jovanny, and perhaps especially little Rory?*

As though these tumbled thoughts weren't already beyond comprehension, what was she to make of the ministrations of both Gage's ex and her boyfriend, victims themselves of whatever it was Gage had done? The *God* and *Jesus* words were coming from the man's lips, not as expletives but reassuringly, almost tenderly. He was speaking in a low but urgent tone to Gage—speaking, unaccountably, of love and forgiveness. The world Mallory had known was slowly heaving itself upside-down.

Daisy

*"Once they know they've got a hold of your shame, they can shake it out and hold it up for all the world to see. And you become less than it. You become something disgusting." —*KIRSTY EAGAR

Mallory didn't know them well, and Gage not at all. But the woman in the next room—Marcella—and her man had been friendly enough over the weeks they'd encountered one another coming and going; Marcella, often outside on the curb dragging a hand-rolled cigarette, chugging a beer, or nursing a soft drink, tended to be gregarious and wide open to chitchat on any subject meandering across her mind. Mallory, lonely during Gage's daytime absences, relished these brief intervals of adult conversation. Marcella and Ed might not be friend material, but shooting the breeze at least in part met a need in Mallory's association-starved soul.

Marcella had been more than gracious in response to Mallory's short-notice need for a sitter, assuring the next-door resident that she and Ed adored kids; the little ones would be in great hands while Mallory and Gage ran to the hospital to see his sick friend.

Daisy, shy by nature and reticent by experience, entered the nearly identical door with misgivings more looming than those likely to trouble a just-seven-year-old mind. Feeling responsible for her brothers, she sat stock still at the foot end of the bed facing the television, holding the fidgety boys with a surprisingly strong-armed firmness, one on either side.

It took no time at all for Ed to express an interest in her presence. Her tight-lipped resolution in response to his repeated insinuations and invitations to join him farther back against the pillows or even in the bathroom (the only closeable door in the tight space) seemed to afford him no end of pleasure, a self-entertainment met on his part with guffaws and leg slapping heard but ignored by his woman.

Tiring at last of this provocation, which was eliciting no response whatsoever, Ed tried to engage the little girl in conversation. This was more problematic for Daisy, who'd been taught to honor her elders by answering when spoken to. "You're a cute little *Cheeeek*anno, a real looker," he observed. "Not like that cheeky golden mama! So what's the other half? What else are ya?" Gleeful at her confusion, he offered suggestions, a string of obviously naughty words that made no sense whatsoever to the dark-eyed child. Finally, in the lowest possible monotone, head bowed, she responded: "Just regular human, I guess."

Ed's authentically surprised response sounded maniacal to the taut little girl, who wished fervently to seep through the floor and disappear. It was at this point that Marcella finally intervened with a curt "Knock it off, Ed! Cain't you see you've got 'er scared off?"

Only moments later Marcella came unexpectedly alive, pointing to the news report on the TV screen and shouting, "Hey, kids, ain't that your ma's old man? Goin' to the hospital to see a friend my eye! Just look at 'im, surrounded by the *pohleece*. Lookit all them cop cars . . . and people. Handcuffs even. And an ambulance. He's got hisself quite an audience, quite an audience."

All three children took in the spectacle with wide-eyed chagrin, having no idea what to make of the scene unfolding before their eyes. But Gage hadn't been arrested, the older children assured themselves; they'd just seen him there at the hotel. He'd been in a hurry and wasn't in his work clothes, but no police were escorting him.

Ed backed off, interested himself in the details of the breaking news story undecipherable to the rigid trio at the foot of the bed. Perhaps the evening held possibilities beyond taunting a rigid seven year old.

Jovanny

*"It is not flesh and blood but the heart which makes
us fathers and sons."* —JOHANN SCHILLER

Old enough to know something was amiss, Jovanny lost no time in informing a wan and preoccupied Gage and Mallory upon their return that Ed was being mean to his sister. No, he hadn't laid a hand on her, but he kept teasing her like a bully. Marcella was okay, but she wasn't a good babysitter if Ed had to be around.

Mallory was to be stunned yet again that day, this time by the intensity of Gage's response to intended abuse involving *her* little girl. Before the night was over Ed's life had indeed taken an interesting turn. In conjunction with the police, hotel management arranged to have the offending resident evicted. There were too many young families in residence to take chances on the establishment's reputation. There would be no charges filed if Ed and Marcella were quick to pack their belongings and be on their way, blacklisted in terms of the possibility of a return. No one in Mallory's recollection had ever expressed anywhere near the level of concern for her that Gage—fresh out of jail himself—just had for Daisy. As she tucked in her precious daughter that night she was overwhelmed by profound gratitude despite her misgivings in the other area.

Jovanny, for his part, swelled with pride. Not only had he effectively stood up for the sister he loved—at some level the little boy recognized her gender disadvantage in terms of adult treatment—but he had galvanized Gage to action on Daisy's behalf. Whatever had happened with Gage that day was and would remain beyond him, but he was beginning to feel a connection with this first man in the family's life to show authentic concern for either mom or kids.

Grant

"Sometimes you break your heart in the right way,
if you know what I mean." —GREGORY DAVID ROBERTS

Morning dawned with positive and rapid change in Luke's outlook. With the resilience typical of the very young, he had awakened during the night and was now weaned of oxygen, talking, and scarfing breakfast before Grant, taking the day off work, arrived in the room. Lauren, flushed with delight, greeted her boyfriend with a wide-armed hug of an intensity that threatened to knock him over. Never before having experienced from her so demonstrative a greeting, he responded in kind, lifting her from the ground and twirling her in a half-circle to accommodate the close quarters. Luke, captivated by his mother's reception of this friendly stranger, broke into delighted giggles. The little boy's vitals were good, and the doctors planned a discharge for later that afternoon, barring any unforeseen complications.

"Official" introductions between Mommy's boy Luke and Mommy's friend Grant pleased the child further. His life to this point had been peopled primarily by women and girls, and the prospect of a new *man* friend of his mom's piqued his interest.

As Grant took in the wholly new perspective of an active, responsive child—*this* dynamic little guy with all his charisma potentially becoming a part of his life—he teared up, turning his head to conceal the over-welling emotion.

He and Lauren, he knew, weren't that far yet; it was still her careful preference to move slowly where the children were concerned. But what he had seen and learned last night, both in the company of Lauren and in the presence of Gage, Mallory, and Adele, had drawn him in deeper. It was becoming apparent that life lived separately from Lauren would be unthinkable. Grant had fallen, and fallen hard . . . and the signs were that all his reasons were right!

Rory

"You don't get explanations in real life. You just get moments that are absolutely, utterly, inexplicably odd." —NEIL GAIMAN

That smaller, flattened version of Gage—except when his face ballooned up for that close-up—had looked less than happy on TV, talking to those miniature policemen in their convincing, tiny uniforms. But Gage was okay now. At least he was back, here in his full-sized flesh. What bothered Rory was how Gage had managed to get himself shrunken into the TV box in Marcella's room in the first place, and why he'd wanted to.

The toddler had wondered many times about this separate sphere mimicking reality and its relationship to the bigger, tangible *truth* he could see and touch all around him. This was the first time in his experience the two had suggested convergence. Rory decided that the closer, three-dimensional reality—the one peopled by the right-size Gage—made sense and felt comfortable. He didn't mind pretending, but when pretense settled in too close to the authentic and known, Rory needed an area of blur.

Adele's Devotion: An August Reading

YOUR WHY

**"'I have come that they may have life,
and have it to the full.'"** (JOHN 10:10)

There are no peripheral human lives—but so many people live their lives so peripherally. It's the difference between functioning as a warm body and being vital and engaged. Do you ever observe an individual or family traipsing re-

signedly through their days with little purpose or dignity and wonder what happened, and when, to beat them down to such a degree?

"God asks no man whether he will accept life," notes Henry Ward Beecher. "That is not the choice. You must take it. The only question is how." Nineteenth-century German philosopher Friedrich Nietzsche focused on that how, while identifying a still more pivotal adverb: "He who has a why to live can bear almost any how." What why drives you? What will you do to share it with someone who is barely bearing their how?

September

Lexie

"Today Teacher took us to music, not art.
I was so embarrassed I put my head in my hands."
"Well, was Mrs. Crenshaw embarrassed?"
"I don't know. She didn't put her head in her hands."

Adele walked the children to school on Lexie's first day of kindergarten. The little girl's tension was palpable—thankfully, it seemed to Adele, more in anticipation than in apprehension. On the trek all three children caught things Adele would have missed. Despite their opening-morning jitters, which affected even Luke, they encountered webs of differing delicacies, including one with its impressive mustard-and-black artist at work. Others shimmered with dewdrops. When Lannie, headed for second grade, wasn't still and absorbed she was skipping, twirling, and calling Adele's attention to other "cool moves." Dandelions tantalized the low-to-the-ground Luke, his fist-clutched bouquet growing for the handoff to Nanna.

Lexie fairly pulsated with nervous energy, determined both to overcome her natural shyness and to make the right impression. Her outfit of choice, a floral dress and sequined red shoes, had been carefully laid out the night before. Glancing around the grassy area before the not yet opened front entrance, she shucked her sunglasses and tiara, shoving them firmly into Adele's hand.

Minutes later Lexie was in motion with some nameless new-found friends. At what point, Adele mused, of awakening maturity does competing or comparing—at least when it comes to bodily movement—become more important than just being? One of the beautiful things about the young, she chuckled, is their disarming lack of inhibition when it comes to trying new things, their lack of awareness of their bodies in space. Adele's timid granddaughter, self-conscious about her speech to the point of choosing much of the time not to engage others in conversation, still moved gracefully in the company of her peers. Observing her in action on the school's front lawn prior to the opening of the double doors, Adele couldn't repress a smile.

Lexie is launched, her nanna thought wryly as she and Luke wended their way homeward in the uncharacteristic coolness, kicking a few early-fallen leaves.

Daisy

"On and on you will hike
and I know you'll hike far
and face up to your problems
whatever they are." —DR. SEUSS

The first day of first grade—never mind it being the second time around. That this time was going to be magical Daisy sensed on her inside, a'tingle with excitement. Mrs. Trumball was there, smiling her wonderful last-year smile Daisy hadn't glanced up often enough to fully appreciate. And Miss Vanessa would be coming, in a couple of weeks, once everybody was off and reading. Daisy had a head start on that one. She knew what to expect, even though it would be different. Because Daisy was different. Ready and not scared. Not even very sad. She allowed herself to glance around the familiar room, not so furtively as on last year's first day. There were other girls, several of whom looked a lot like herself. Maybe girls she could help, like Mrs. Trumball had suggested last year. She ventured a trial smile—just a little one—at a promising one two rows over. And the girl she chose smiled back, friendly as could be.

Gage

> *"Only those who are truly aware of their sin can truly cherish grace."* —C. J. MAHONEY

Gage seemed wholly unable to account for the roundabout manner in which he had sought audience with his children, when he could reasonably have contacted Lauren by phone to convince her that he had changed and deserved another chance. Her unlikely consent wouldn't have allowed a breaking of the PPO, but he could possibly have convinced her to rescind the order. It was apparent that a guilt-induced, felt lack of entitlement had nudged him in the illegal direction.

For the second time within a year Gage had made, and continued off and on for more than a month following the incident to make, the news—this time not as a tall, blonde, lightweight-beige-jacket-clad threat to local children but as the unlikely "hero" in a bizarre human interest story evidently moving in the direction of a happy ending. Given the reason for the little boy's presence at the lake in the first place, public opinion had wavered initially. But Lauren's willingness to rescind the personal protection order, which also made the news, along with more and more detail coming to light, turned the tide of opinion in Gage's favor. The story of the infant's death (the investigation by the authorities in North Carolina collaborated the couple's rendition by failing to turn up evidence of foul play), in conjunction with Gage's part in saving Luke's life, in fact generated an outpouring of sympathy and assistance for Gage and Mallory and her kids.

Gage's supervised meeting with his own children was postponed till a little later in the fall, pending the outcome of sentencing, which might well include incarceration. In the meantime, the court-ordered provision for repeal of the PPO already mandated Gage's involvement in AA. Though he had seen himself in no danger of relapsing again despite the trauma of the past months, he was happy, with Mallory's relieved support, to comply.

The willingness of both Lauren and Adele to forgive served as a shining example to Gage of the forgiveness and grace God too was prepared to lavish on him. The members of his new family took their cue from him in this regard. They were seeing a changed man and were lured by both curiosity and desire to follow in his footsteps.

The family's attendance at an informal neighborhood church service in the vicinity of the hotel was met with a warm welcome; if anyone recognized them from the news coverage—which must have been the case—no one let on. This experience, though familiar to Gage from his early years with Lauren, was new to Mallory and her children, all of whom responded guardedly to the unaccustomed inclusion.

Adele

"I am somewhat exhausted; I wonder how a battery feels when it pours electricity into a non-conductor." —ARTHUR CONAN DOYLE

Dinner was in progress, the three women and three children surrounding the oval table bent over early-autumn "comfort" plates of chili, cheese, and crackers. Typical of September's sporadic weather patterns, the day had been warm and humid, but the fare still felt appropriate. "Look!" Lannie squealed without preamble. Five heads rose in unison, and five additional pairs of eyes locked on a spectacle unfolding inches from their faces. A single strand from an unseen web had dropped from a blade of the ceiling fan whirling above the table, and its dun brown occupant, still clinging tenaciously to this lifeline, was being whipped around. Too surprised at this absurd exhibition to turn off the fan, Adele and Lauren broke the silence by laughter. The three little ones and Nadine, opting in kind for humor as opposed to fear, gave in to merriment.

At that moment an equally unforeseen development sobered

even the little ones: the spider began methodically to inch its way back up the strand—all the way up to the blade from which it had plummeted.

That spider, Adele conceded in respect, had spunk. In addition, that single strand of her web had held remarkably well against the centrifugal force working against it. Yet, unaccountably, Adele's overriding response was one of exhaustion. Watching that slow and deliberate progress—in the long run, to what end?—made her feel for the moment more tired than inspired.

Rory

"We are driven by five genetic needs; survival, love and belonging, power, freedom, and fun." —WILLIAM GLASSER

The inundation of communal generosity following the intriguing news coverage and revelation of the family's plight was met with full-out enthusiasm on the part of the two year old. Rory, having set eyes and hands on relatively few real toys within his short life, suddenly found himself not knowing what to play with first. Mallory wisely squirreled away most of the options, allowing each child to become acquainted with a manageable number of choices. Other toys were boxed and labeled with an eye toward future birthdays and boredom and Christmas.

The constraints of the hotel room no longer seemed to rankle, as each child managed to claim a private corner. Beeps and vrooms and squealing brakes and ongoing "two-way" conversations during schooldays replaced the din of endless cartoons, pronouncing Rory overwhelmed by stimuli. Mallory couldn't help but smile as she went about organizing, storing, and planning. The space was blessed to overflowing—and that didn't count its human occupants!

A change was called for, as she and Gage discussed endlessly in whispered voices in their bed, aware that the severity of Gage's sentencing might negate any hope of near-term possibilities. Mallory's dream centered around three bedrooms, at long last giving

Daisy a place of her own. The rent for a two-bedroom already prohibitive, though, they acknowledged that this criterion might have to be negotiable.

Nadine

"The closer we come to understanding the challenges of autism, the better we are placed to accommodate . . . without risking removing the individuality we all love." —ADELE DEVINE

Nadine's action of holding Luke's head underwater prompted a comprehensive, court-ordered psychological evaluation yielding much information about her sister's condition of which Adele had never been aware. Identification of autism as a disorder with a name and predictable set of characteristics had occurred long after Nadine and Adele's shared childhood. Yet despite the in-depth current interest in and research into the syndrome, the details for Adele were little more than interesting. Nadine had intended no more harm in "helping" Luke hide than Gage had in arranging for her to lure the children to the park—though he was certainly culpable in a way she could never be!

The vigilance and unconditional love Adele had known for her sister since her own first sentient months of life were unwavering; the well-intentioned suggestion of "other arrangements" for Nadine was passed off without serious thought. Adele and Nadine, together through virtually all of Adele's life, would remain a twosome for as long as circumstances allowed.

Grant

"Sometimes good things fall apart so better things can fall together."
—MARILYN MONROE

Grant's meeting with the girls (Luke already accepted him as a buddy from his hospital introduction) was to be a big moment for both Lauren and her boyfriend. Prior to the meeting the couple had discussed each of the children in detail, to the point that

Grant felt he already knew them. Though he had never fathered a child, his comfort level with kids was high, in part on the basis of his own childhood in an overflowing house and later immersion in the lives of nephews and nieces. At this point, however, he was to be introduced on a first-name basis simply as Momma's friend from school. A Saturday noon picnic at the park was planned.

The children, in preparation, were in high spirits, as was Grant, though he tamped down his enthusiasm in light of a degree of nervous anxiety he'd detected during the week in Lauren. This was a side of her he'd seldom seen, though he felt he understood her dis-ease. Lauren, Grant rightly surmised, had no reservations about him personally but understood that the stakes were high. Her children had been hurt once by the breakdown of a marriage, and the prospect of traumatizing or even disappointing them weighed on her. To complicate the situation, the *other* meeting—the one between Gage and the three—was tentatively planned to take place within weeks, pending the outcome of sentencing. How was Lauren in the long run to differentiate these two emergent daddies in her children's minds? How was she to ensure their attachment to Grant in light of possible competition from, or loyalty to, Gage?

Shortly before noon the family of four sallied from the house with their picnic basket for the short walk. Turning into the park at the green bench, Lauren caught sight of a waving Grant rising from his perch atop a picnic table and walking toward them with a studied nonchalance. The three children, understanding this to be Momma's school friend, broke into a run to meet him. Lannie and Luker, who was already comfortable with Grant, took his hands, tugging him to move faster toward Momma, with Lexie predictably holding back in assessment mode.

Introductions, though made, were superfluous; the girls understood that Momma's friend Grant was joining them for a picnic, and Grant obviously had no questions about who they were. Within minutes even the cautious Lexie had been drawn in.

Less than two hours later, a tuckered Luke in need of a nap, five strolled down the sidewalk toward the house. Though Grant and Adele were comfortable together, this was to be his introduction to Aunt Nadine, as well as to Lauren's childhood home.

He returned to the park for his car half an hour later, anticipation soaring. As he'd expected, he was head over heels not only for Lauren but also for her—no, *their*—three lovely children.

Lannie

"There are worse things to do when you're in grade two than to spend your time building a dream." —ANDREA BEATY

Lannie's active mind had places to go and things to engage. Sometimes her thoughts converged with what Miss Van Hout happened to be saying in class, especially if it was interesting, sometimes not. Usually she managed to pick up on what she'd missed through its repetition, via intuition, or by association. Miss Van Hout, she learned, was patient, but she had expectations too—high ones. That fact in itself captured Lannie's fancy; it didn't take long before her hopes and dreams began to merge with her teacher's desires for her.

Jovanny

"[Y]our children need to be taught God's truth—by you. They will not absorb it by osmosis or by breathing the air in your home. They will not become convicted of God's truth by default." —JIM SERVIDIO

Unlike their mother or, to a much greater extent, Gage, Mallory's children had no prior exposure to God or faith. One Sunday morning in church, seated with his family in the last row of chairs, Jovanny attempted to make sense of the experience. Finding it difficult to catch sight of the talking head up front, the little boy finally appealed to Gage: *"Please pick me up! I can't see God!"*

Jovanny's innocent plea stayed with Gage in the days to follow. While the responsibility he was assuming for Mallory's children at times weighed on him, he hadn't viewed himself as accountable to them—or to her—from a spiritual standpoint. Nor was this a matter of his being a new initiate. Gage's experience with God and faith was relatively extensive—had even at times in the past been intensive.

Gage knew, understood, and believed. His reluctance to come clean with God during much of the past decade had been guilt-induced and, at bottom, selfish. Despite head-knowledge of a forgiving God, Gage hadn't been willing to let go of his self-pride by acknowledging his inability to pull *himself* up to his assumed standard of righteousness.

There was nothing wrong with the standard, he now recognized, . . . except that it wasn't God's. Oh, God the Father was all for holiness, but the degree of goodness a Christian might attain—*was expected by God to attain*—was all about Christ's *gift* of salvation and, with it, forgiveness and sanctification. The grateful believer responded in love with service, a natural outgrowth of belief. But to try to circumvent the gift, to declare it inadequate by attempting to work around it on one's own—that was a slap in God's face.

In the days and weeks before sentencing this realization troubled Gage a good deal. The fallacy of his earlier "take" on these issues seemed so obvious now. Gage had—and continued to, in other areas of his life—come clean with God. Now the burden of his responsibility to family was taking on an unprecedented urgency. He owed Jovanny, *now*, a complete, if basic, explanation, an airlift to catch sight of the true God, the loving, forbearing Father.

Luke

"There is no despair so absolute as that which comes with our first great sorrow." —GEORGE ELLIOT

During the summer the three children, Adele, and Nadine had enjoyed a viewing of *Bambi*. Adele had hoped her grandson would handle the loss of the fawn's mother without anything close to real comprehension, and he did seem unaffected. She'd opted to skip over the fire scene, choosing to "end" the movie after Bambi, Thumper, and Flower had been twitterpated.

On a Friday evening in September Lauren decided to treat the kids to the same movie, unaware of their earlier exposure. She shared with Adele afterward Luke's unexpected behavior when the storyline neared the time of the doe's death. Her son had become highly agitated, first attempting to cover the screen with his arms and hands. This proving only partially success-ful, he had begun turning the power off and on again until the dreaded scene had safely passed. Lauren, recalling Adele's earlier concern about Lexie's exposure to violent death from adult TV, was finally convicted.

Mallory

"In the end, . . . maybe we must all give up trying to pay back the people in this world who sustain our lives. In the end, maybe it's wiser to surrender before the miraculous scope of human generosity and just keep saying thank you, forever and sincerely, for as long as we have voices." —ELIZABETH GILBERT

When it came to gratitude, Mallory didn't know where to direct it, how to express it, or even where to begin. Truth was, she'd had little experience with needing to address these issues. Now she had the bewildering feeling that, no matter where she turned, some anonymous good person was smiling on her, deserving her thanks. Perhaps a smile accidently directed at the right individ-ual would find its mark. At any rate, suppressing the happiness welling up within was becoming more difficult. And why should she try?

It was apparent that Gage loved the change in her, and the children were both mystified and thrilled. Daisy wanted noth-ing more than to be seen with her beautiful mama, and the boys walked a little taller in her presence. Underneath and above it all—and despite her anxiety over the unknowns surrounding Gage's coming court date—Mallory cherished her secret, pondering it like Mary in her quiet moments; the life growing within her this time—and at this time—seemed right, despite her uncertainty, in so many ways. The very air seemed pregnant with promise. And she would savor it alone for just a little while longer . . .

Lauren

"Life can only be understood backwards; but it must be lived forwards." —SOREN KIERKEGAARD

In light of the year's developments, both Lauren and Grant felt it best to take a semester, or possibly even a year, off night school. Their hope was that Grant would be able, possibly after their first year of marriage, to begin a more intensive course of study, while Lauren would continue in her present position at the hotel; a coming offer of promotion to a management position had already been hinted. Her ambivalence about the field with which she'd been toying, architecture, played in to the decision from her side. Lauren recognized in hindsight her own mixed motivations for returning to school in the first place: part boredom, or maybe it was restlessness; part a desire to be less hands-on for a time with the children, in light of their residence in Adele's home; part a social tug, though many of the evening students were closer to the traditional college age; and part an open-ended desire for learning.

A further consideration was Grant's expressed desire for biological fatherhood—not immediately, but not in the too distant future either. Neither he nor Lauren had reached the mid-thirties mark, but they felt it best not to extend for too long the age difference between Luke and his brother- or sister-to-be. Neither would necessarily have opted for more than three children, but together they accepted that the circumstances stretched a bit beyond the ordinary.

Adele's Devotion: A September Reading

THE EMBRACE

**"He stretches out the heavens like a canopy,
and spreads them out like a tent to live in."** (ISAIAH 40:22)

I enjoyed an article recently by a Christian mom whose daughter's junior kindergarten teacher had invited the children to experiment with the styles and techniques of a variety of artists. One little boy, having imitated Michelangelo's painting on the ceiling of the Sistine Chapel (he had lain on his back with his "canvas" taped to the underside of a table), observed, "I'm happy to see my own painting on the ceiling. . . . I feel like I'm in heaven hugging God."

Our God is a ceiling painter too. His gallery is panoramic, breathtaking, and open 24/7 for all to enjoy, free of charge. And his renditions are endless and ever changing; we have only to lift our gaze at any hour of any day in any season to feel ourselves enveloped in his embrace. A prelude of sorts, I suppose, for an eternity "up there," . . . hugging God back.

October

Grant

*"God created us in his image, male and female, with
personhood and sexual passions, so that when he comes to us
in this world there would be these powerful words and images
to describe the promises and the pleasures of our covenant
relationship with him through Christ."* —JOHN PIPER

No, the ring wouldn't be a surprise, not in the sense that it was
coming. That decision, which had needed to be mutual, had
been talked out earnestly, beginning months earlier. The couple's shared commitment to the Lord, each other, and the children, in that order, had been confirmed one to another in what
amounted to early vows. Lauren, not one for fuss, had expressed a
preference for a simple, low-key ceremony, an intimate family affair. The date had been set for January 9, 2015, a little more than
a week after the busy holidays, with Grant's dad officiating. The
location was to be a small annex—a chapel-like setting—in Lauren's church (which was soon to become Grant's as well).

The practical Lauren preferred to forego a diamond in favor of
a heftier down payment on a home, but Grant overrode her on that
score. He had postponed marriage into his thirties and was going
to get this part right! Always an avid window-shopper, Lauren had
accompanied him to several jewelry stores, invariably gravitating
toward the least expensive; this was enough for her husband-to-be
to clarify her taste. With his mother's help he had settled on an

elegant setting along the line of a style she had pointed out.

The ring in its box was nestled in his jacket pocket this mid-October afternoon as he and Lauren wandered the neighborhood, accompanied by the crunch of leaves. Grant, charmed by Lannie's designation of the semicircular road skirting the park along the wooded side, strolled naturally in the direction of the wiggle road. The afternoon was pristine and the color at its peak, the palette from the park side breathtakingly. The diamond, Grant couldn't help but assess, paled in comparison on this day to God's spendthrift outlay, the lake a mirror image at ground level of the beauty still mantling the maples. A location that could have signified tragedy instead elicited in both a humble gratitude.

Rory

"God does not suffer presumption in anyone but himself." —HERODOTUS

The children played together in a corner of the cramped hotel room; in anticipation of a move, though the details remained uncertain, the luxury of separate toy stashes and corners had temporarily been given up, the space given over to piles of packed and labeled boxes. Daisy bent over her Barbies, graciously allowing her brothers to share the dolls, clothing, and accessories littering the floor.

Rory crouched across from her on his haunches, wielding a Ken doll in gargantuan movements. At almost three still lacking a handle on size differentiation, he paused upon noting Gage's loafers within reach and proudly stood Ken in the big shoes, unfazed by the proportional discrepancy. The blonde doll stood erect and tall, master of the situation. It was Jovanny who objected in his usual diplomatic manner: "He's going to trip, and he can't pick up his feet. He's going to bump stuff and step on people."

"Them's God's shoes," Rory announced contemplatively, backing off slightly to access the incongruity for the first time. "I know cuz they're too big."

Gage

*"Christianity is not primarily a moral code
but a grace-laden mystery; it is not essentially
a philosophy of love but a love affair; it is not keeping rules
with clenched fists but receiving a gift with
open hands."* —BRENNAN MANNING

When the October court date arrived, Gage was sentenced to a $2,000 fine, probation (including the wearing of an ankle tether), community service, and a requirement for counseling, in addition to his continued participation in AA, already in place as a stipulation for the repeal of the PPO. No provision was made or planned for unsupervised visits with his children, although the future was open-ended in this regard.

Given what Gage saw as the stigma of his criminal record and probation, an offer came from his perspective out of the blue. A man approached the couple after a Sunday morning service, introducing himself as the owner of a local auto repair shop who found himself in need of a reliable mechanic. Given Gage's initiation in his present job, it had occurred to him that he might be interested—job training to be a part of the package.

Despite the overtures on the part of both the community and, more recently, the church, the possibility of being *approached* with a job offer floored both Gage and Mallory. This unforeseen change in employment status would brighten their prospects immensely.

But more was to come. Evidently some networking on the family's behalf among the church community had been going on. The next surprise, equally as incomprehensible, came only days later with an offer from a landlord—a member of the deacon board—of a two-bedroom, second-story apartment in an older home at a more than reasonable rent. The living room, he explained, included a recessed alcove of sorts that from his wife's perspective would, when curtained or otherwise partitioned off, make an adorable little girl's room with its window seat and closet.

He would paint to their specifications prior to the move-in, the matter of a couple of days' work with help from the youth group. The older couple living on the ground floor were open to children, and full use of the yard would be the family's, in exchange for lawn mowing, leaf raking, and snow shoveling by Gage.

For Mallory in particular, nearing her second trimester in a new pregnancy (*not a replacement!* she and Gage mutually agreed), the timing couldn't have been more auspicious. She'd been holding back a little on the God thing, she had to acknowledge—a wait and see testing of sorts—but couldn't help but be overawed by the circumstances lining up like dominoes—not ready to fall, as she was accustomed, but to fall into place. No, circumstances probably wouldn't always pan out this way, she and Gage recognized, but for the time being—just when they needed it—the *God of love* was coming through, along with his people, with flying colors. At some future point, they promised one another, it would be their time to give!

Lexie

"Momma, I love you forty-ninety-ninety-ninety-ninety-ninety times. How much do you love me?"

Lauren struggled with Lexie over the wording of some kindergarten "parent homework." Asked to explain why Lexie was "the apple of her eye," Lauren jotted down phrase after phrase. Adele encouraged her daughter not to overthink the assignment, throwing out some simple samples, not necessarily intended to fit the situation, like "She's my best friend." Lexie cut in, contesting earnestly, "Momma isn't my best friend. I just love her."

Lauren, moved, realized that she tended to view her second daughter as being closer to Adele than to herself. Her feelings of entitlement to this child had been curtailed by circumstances, and she had reluctantly given in to considering Adele Lexie's surrogate mom. Life with Gage had been much more problematic by the time this second one had come around, and Lauren's unhappiness at the time had done little to bolster the bonding process. With two daughters only eighteen months apart and an unreliable husband to contend with, Lauren had found it necessary to enter the workforce within six weeks of this second birth. She recognized now how guilt-inducing this "choice" had actually been.

Gazing now into her middle child's serious blue eyes, Lauren was overcome with the force of an unrestrained reciprocal love she had never before permitted herself to acknowledge.

Lauren

"We have, as human beings, a storytelling problem.
We're a bit too quick to come up with explanations
for things we don't really have an explanation for."
—MALCOLM GLADWELL

The children's "official" reunion with their dad was scheduled to take place over lunch at a family restaurant with only Lauren, Gage, and the three kids present. For Lannie this would be primarily a matter of catching up, and Lexie retained an inkling of memory. Luke, unconscious in August when Gage had first seen him, would be meeting his daddy for the first time.

Lauren prepared the children ahead of time without making too big a deal of the lunch date. To the girls' questions about Gage's appearance in August, she commented in language they would understand on how providential it had been for their very own dad to happen upon his family exactly when they needed him. Daddy knew, she explained, that Aunt Nadine was just playing and meant no harm in holding Luke's head under the water, but he also understood that boys and girls need to hold their breath when the swim and can only do that for a little while. Daddy wasn't being mean to Aunt Nadine—they'd been friends for a very long time, since way before Lannie was born. He'd had to be rough with her at the park because sometimes she didn't understand things in the same way other people did. The girls nodded solemnly, knowing this to be the case.

Now Daddy was anxious to get to know his kids again. He had loved them all along but hadn't known where to find them after Momma and Daddy were no longer married. Lexie nodded unquestioningly, while the better-informed Lannie, who knew Daddy had once lived in Nanna's house, decided it best for now not to voice her rash of questions. Grownup life got way too complicated sometimes; what mattered is that she'd missed Daddy and would welcome his reintroduction into her life.

Lannie

"I just hope God does not get bored of dreaming me."
—AUTHOR UNKNOWN

"Look at this, Nanna" (holding up a Play-Doh sculpture). "It's a finished touch!"

"Not like us." Adele's provocative answer (her smiling face turned toward the stove) was intended to elicit a response— and did.

"I'm *done*" (looking over fingers and glancing down at feet), " . . . butcept getting taller" (there had to be a catch).

"I'm growing too."

"No!" (carefully, not wanting to be embarrassed by a *gotcha!*). "You're already big."

"I'm growing inside, in my heart and mind and soul. God's work in us is never done!"

"Me too!" Lannie's seven-year-old face, flashing a decidedly more grownup smile than even a month earlier, was filling in, Adele noticed with a smile, to accommodate her new and so adult front teeth.

Mallory

*"An infinite God can give all of Himself to each
of His children. He does not distribute Himself that each*

may have a part, but to each one He gives all of Himself
*as fully as if there were no others." —*A. W. TOZER

Mallory's delight in the new apartment knew no bounds. Her second trimester had been her high-energy period with all four previous pregnancies, and this one was no exception. After months of confinement and tedium—not to mention devastation—in a restrictive environment not her own, she found herself overcome with thankfulness. The very street with its quaint older homes nearly butted up against one another, except for the at-times intervening driveways; the steeply sloping front yards with their echoing sets of railed stairs; the maples clad in fall color lining the street and partially overlaying it from above; the rippling eddies of not-yet-dried leaves blowing randomly before being trapped in some corner—all alike intrigued her, pulling her back in imagination to some idyllic yesterday she'd never personally experienced.

The apartment, vintage 1920–1930, was in excellent repair; fresh paint, as promised, echoed the couple's personal choices, and period details, though not extravagant, held charm for any appreciative resident. Like a crisp white sheet overlaying a used mattress, the experience to some degree overspread the grief Mallory continued to carry from earlier in the year. No, that anguish wasn't buried—truth was, she wouldn't have wanted it that way—but the new enchantments tamped down the preoccupation, letting it rest.

The empty apartment was for Mallory a blank canvas, an already beautiful backdrop begging for enhancement. Her enthusiasm was matched by her daughter's; Daisy and her mama had never before shared a passion, but this was it.

The packed and labeled boxes from August and September had made the short trip via the landlord's pickup, along with the family's clothing, toys, and personal items. An eclectic mix of furniture, kitchen and cleaning necessities, even sheets and towels, all donated by church members, arrived within the hour by U-Haul, followed by a raucous carload of enthusiastic teens, also care of the church. Mallory and Gage would carefully budget for whatever might still be needed; that would be half the fun.

The little boys saw potential too, though their gaze over-looked—or rather looked beyond—the aesthetics. As they had so briefly down South, the two made short work of exploring every corner, indoors and out, including the unused garage facing the narrow alley that split the block, and the backyard shed. No mountainside came with this package, but the opportunities seemed as inexhaustible. Gage took stock of the yard equipment, sorry the lawn mowing would wait till April. He and his boys would soon enough tackle the raking—an experience they would mutually enjoy.

Mallory and Daisy took delight in directing the youth group volunteers in placement of the items emerging one by one up the enclosed staircase and through the "front" door. Daisy reveled this time around in the appreciative mama at her side, a mama laughing and exclaiming and agreeing and applauding her decorating ideas. Was it just possible that life, already good, could *improve*?

Luke

"You don't choose your family. They are God's gift to you, as you are to them." —DESMOND TUTU

Luke, watching an episode of his favorite cartoon, *Caillou*, from the carpet, arms hugging bent knees, rocked back and forth as effectively as Aunt Nadine, behind him in her rocker—but without the creak. Nanna's bobbing head had just disappeared into the basement stairwell, bound for the laundry room—an ordinary October Monday morning in progress, its familiarity a comfort to the routine-thriving pair in the living room. It was the cessation of the rhythmic creak that prompted the little boy to turn around for a backward glance.

Aunt Nadine, no longer in rocking mode, was acting strangely, so strangely her appreciative audience burst into laughter before checking himself, puzzled. Her pumping foot was silent, but the rest of her body shook unnaturally—how did she *do* that?—and her facial features contorted in a grimace altogether unlike a smile. Her eyes, wide open, were unseeing, her teeth clenched, and a thin rope of saliva coming from the crack where her lips met stretched itself down, attaching to her shirt. His great-aunt was making noises, but they were unfamiliar—animal grunts that caught even Arabelle's attention.

Luke, uncertain, stood and edged closer, as though his reassuring presence might help her change her mind about this display. Sometimes Aunt Nadine surprised him, but she usually appreciated the joke as much as he did once he caught on. Drawing closer, he helped her rock until a semblance of normalcy resumed. His great-aunt was still now, though neither talking nor laughing. Luke climbed into her lap, facing her; pushed an arm behind her back; and lay quietly, head against her chest, allowing her to absorb his hug. It was here that Nanna found them a short time later, both asleep.

Adele

"The most precious etchings of caring can be traced not in the scope of its message, but in the integrity of its purpose." —JOHNATHAN JENA

Late October and early November is the time in West Michigan when the leaves get serious about falling. Walking to school with the children, Adele was struck by the "precipitation" from individual trees. Passing one yard she commented to the little ones on the interesting leaf formations on the grass. Beneath the red and yellow trees, respectively, lay almost perfectly rounded mantles of colored leaves, the perimeters of the circles barely overlapping at one point. For the moment that lawn was a mosaic of carefully laid-out color.

Each of those trees, she mused, had its own unique circle, its own beauty manifested in its own place. But what intrigued her this morning was that area of overlap, or overlay. That football of mingled color signified to her the spot within which she could exert some real influence. Gage and Mallory and her—no, *their*—children came immediately to mind. The lives of two families, parts of which had for a long time been one, were converging in a way that seemed positive and right, with no foreseeable vulnerability for those she loved. A melding into a single circle of caring, and even love, seemed right, and she would do what she could to promote it.

Care and its giving had played a pivotal role in Adele's life, though never as a vocation, for as far back as she could remember. But always there'd been that pull for more—more inclusivity, more intentionality, . . . and more gratitude as their impetus. Still, she was slowing down and knew it, her "Go for it!" mentality beginning to allow for some restrictive clauses. Not "outs" as such, but inklings of realism that tempered the habitual "all out" enthusiasm of her intentions. Adele would do what she could with this family too to welcome and promote and encourage. But "what she could" today was a little more sensible, a little more realistic, than what she'd chosen some two years earlier for Lauren and her three.

Daisy

"Yesterday is history, tomorrow is a mystery, today is a gift of God, which is why we call it the present." —BIL KEANE

The first-grade vision screening came earlier this year; Daisy had been missed during the last school year due to her absence in North Carolina. Both Jovanny and Daisy (first-graders in different classes), it was found, needed glasses, though Daisy's vision problems were more significant than her brother's.

In addition, she had been tested early in the year for possible dyslexia, resulting in regular tutoring provided within the building through the school system. Daisy liked both her one-on-one teacher and her pretty new glasses; she was one of several in the classroom to have "sprouted" them—free of charge, though she didn't know it—over a single weekend. Not only did she not feel singled out, she was amazed at the ability of those lenses to curtail the jumping of the letters and numbers. Life in general was going way better, just as Mrs. Trumball had predicted.

Nadine

"Normal people think we're highly dependent and can't live without ongoing support, but in fact there are times when we're stoic heroes." —NAOKI HIGASHIDA

Following her first known seizure, witnessed by Luke and Arabelle—neither of whom could relate the experience to Adele—Nadine's decline was steep. Ironically, one of her areas of greatest dependability throughout her six plus decades had been her excellent health. Despite her deficits in other areas, she'd been endowed with a seemingly iron constitution, allowing her to avoid or slough off many of those communicable illnesses that laid other family members low. "Always blessed . . . "

The diagnosis in late October of an inoperable stage-four malignant brain tumor evoked in Adele a bittersweet response. Her sister's pain could be managed, and the duration would be blessedly short—two to four months was the prognosis. In the meantime a hospital bed found pride of place in the living room, home hospice care commenced, and the invalid took center stage, quite literally, in family life. All three children found opportunity at one time or another to curl up with her in the fascinating bed that reclined at different angles, "reading" or singing or prattling. Nadine remained aware and responsive throughout, except when the seizures or pain medication blurred her reality, although she spoke less and less often or coherently.

"Caregiving often calls us to lean into love we didn't know possible." —TIA WALKER

Her sister's continual need took its toll on Adele, forcing her to relinquish all activities that involved leaving home except during the availability of Lauren or the visiting nurse. Lannie and

Lexie were escorted to and from school by a helpful neighbor with school children of her own. At least once weekly Lauren and Grant arranged a date in the living room, surrounded by the flurry of activity, now including homework for two, denoting a busy young family. Despite this opportunity for shopping or coffee out, Adele most often excused herself to her room for some uninterrupted quiet; she was often asleep before the children settled in for the night.

Jovanny

"It's the children the world almost breaks who grow up to save it." —FRANK WARREN

He stood there atop the slide, petrified to proceed and unable due to the line behind him to retrace the rungs in a backward direction. For this kindergartner with Downs Syndrome, the steps that had looked so inviting morphed at their top into a terrifying drop-off; the perspective from above was deceptively different from that below. The patience of the little ones was admirable; baffled by the unforeseen dilemma and not wishing to hurt, not one ventured a word. The only voice came from the playground supervisor, who had planted herself at the bottom, beckoning encouragement with outstretched arms and waving fingers.

In the end it was Jovanny, directly behind Talon in line, who broke the stalemate. Whispering in Talon's ear, he began to gingerly lift and guide the boy's frozen limbs, one at a time, into a sitting posture, after which he eased himself into position behind him, his skinny legs around Talon's as in a hug. Jovanny didn't push off till he was certain the other boy was on board. Without attempting to trick or coerce, Jovanny prepared his schoolmate for the adventure before them. Waiting for the nod, which was barely perceptible, Jovanny began the inchmeal descent, using his rubber soles as brakes.

Not surprisingly, Talon was overawed, at the experience of sliding and by his first encounter with a school friend. For the rest of that recess, and for other noon recesses to follow, Jovanny and Talon joined the line at the slide again and again for their joint ride. Other children took their cue, so that Talon was never unattended during the midmorning kindergarten recess either. Until he was ready a little later to take the plunge on his own, whichever child happened to be behind him in line assumed position for the doubles drop.

Adele's Devotion: An October Reading

FAITH IN THE DARK

"Now faith is confidence in what we hope for and assurance about what we do not see." (HEBREWS 11:1)

William Newton Clark put it this way: "Faith is daring the soul to go beyond what the eyes can see." There's no mention of darkness in either definition, but the image that comes naturally to me is one of groping. For us as sighted creatures there can be little more disconcerting than to strain our pupils against a lack of light. And in many cases nothing more courageous than to push forward anyway.

To what degree does your faith manifest itself in the context of darkness? Is it most active and evident then, or does it threaten to founder, retreating into the shadows waiting for a resurgence of illumination? Confidence and assurance, like other faith "muscles," need to be exercised in order to thrive. And effective exercise happens best in demanding conditions.

November

Lexie

"Practicing the presence of God will make us good at it."
—F. ALAN WOODS

Lexie seemed to have shucked her recent fixation with death and bad guys and replaced it with a keen awareness of God's presence—her recently acquired understanding of "invisible" fascinated her, evidently affording a degree of comfort and confidence. In the car on a late-afternoon errand, Lexie and Adele explored synonyms to describe the overcast day: "cloudy" versus "dark," "windy" versus "blustery" (Lexie preferred the latter, based on its familiarity from a Winnie the Pooh book). Moments later the pulsing sun infiltrated a break in the clouds, transforming the landscape on its underside. Taken aback, she marveled, "That looks like heaven, Nanna—*I think I just saw God!*"

A few days later, during one of those transitional half hours rapidly cycling from rain to sleet to snow, Adele, gazing out the picture window, made the rather inane comment, "There's something in the air, and it isn't exactly snow." Lexie, turning around briefly from her floor play, prompted helpfully, "Maybe God?"

Gage

"So much of what is best in us is bound up in our love of family, that it remains the measure of our stability because it

measures our sense of loyalty. All other pacts of love or fear
derive from it and are modeled upon it." —DANIEL LONG

Like Lauren's to come, Gage's second union was to be a low-key, family affair. The intention had been a justice-of-the-peace ceremony, but the family's new pastor, Kent, had enthusiastically offered to officiate. Adele, Lauren, Grant, and the children were to be in attendance in the church fellowship hall; a friend would sit at home with Aunt Nadine. Kent's wife, Gage's boss, the family's landlord, and their wives would complete the intimate gathering. Modest refreshments would be supplied by the church's fellowship committee.

Lannie

"Autumn is a season of desperate hopes. The leaves
are souls begging to turn life on pause. Begging to
stop, begging to take a break." —TEODORA SAVU

Adele, a faithful Lannie at her side, found herself again this year struggling with an unwelcome late-autumn ritual, raking crispy-leaves-turned-soggy in the toe- and finger-chilling grass under a light November rain. This was hardly their first foray into the yard this fall, but waiting for those last leaves, which had let go of their color before their tenacious hold, frustrated Adele, knowing as she did the conditions under which they'd be finishing the task. No, it hadn't all been left to the two of them. Lauren, both alone and with Lannie and/or Grant, had done her share, but those trees seemed to yield an endless number of filled leaf bags. And the wetter or more icy the leaves, the heavier the bags. This day Adele found herself tight-lipped and miserable, vowing to herself that this would be her last year of hefting these loads.

Lannie, addressing the stack of plastic bags filled a few days earlier, on a blessedly dry afternoon, had more enterprising thoughts on her mind. "Nanna," she reflected, "If we dump out some of these, it will make the soil taste more much better for plants."

"Great idea!" returned Adele, less enthused than her granddaughter but appreciating the gesture. "We'll get some of those in the garden before winter."

How she appreciated this unflappable sidekick! Lannie, the ever eager, was becoming more a boon to her nanna than a responsibility!

Mallory

"If I get married, I want to be very married." —AUDREY HEPBURN

Lauren shopped with Mallory for her dress and shoes, the two brides-to-be giddy with mutual anticipation. Mallory (still barely showing) chose a simple, knee-length aqua chemise with jacket—her favorite color—with an understated chain and earrings and off-white, low-heeled shoes. Despite the season, matching dresses in complementary pastels were selected—all of the children's clothing Grant's gift—for the three little girls. The three boys would also coordinate in khaki slacks, contrasting sweater vests over pastel shirts in different colors, and ties. The ever-practical Lauren would repurpose her children's outfits for her own and Grant's coming nuptials.

A hair and nails appointment for Mallory and haircuts for all six children followed a day or two later, a la Lauren; elaborate braiding of Daisy's long, silken tresses was scheduled for the morning of. Lauren's three, by now accustomed to their status as members of dual families—had accepted Mallory's as siblings, and a family portrait—to be taken at the wedding—to include Gage, Mallory, and all six—was already planned for the couple's living room. Lauren and Grant would maintain full custody of Lannie, Lexie, and Luke, with visits, though frequent, involving both families.

Though Lauren alone had been previously married, Mallory's approach to her wedding was less idealistic—fully as anticipated but without the newness, the mystery aspect. The love between her and Gage had seasoned and mellowed almost before she had acknowledged it; in fact, it had come to her as something of a hindsight wonder—something she had neither expected nor been able at first to identify. The two had lived through so much together that, despite a history of disadvantages and setbacks, a surprising maturity had come to characterize their union. Or was it a surprising unity in their dawning maturity?

Daisy

"Instruction does much, but encouragement everything." —JOHANN WOLFGANG VON GOETHE

Neither Mrs. Trumball nor Vanessa could get over the change in Daisy. Certainly a second year in the first grade was doing her no harm, and the new glasses seemed to pop everything into perspective for the little girl in terms of the puzzle that had been the typeset page. Not only had Daisy's reading ability taken off, but her personality, in comparison to the stifled, tentative child of the year before, was blossoming. She was making eye contact of her own initiative and, though still quiet, was liked by the other children and becoming a sought-after friend. It was in large part the success stories like hers that made both women's endeavors feel so rewarding!

Nadine

"Just by looking at nature, I feel as if I'm being swallowed up into it, and in that moment I get the sensation that my body is now a speck, a speck from long before I was born, a speck that is melting into nature itself." —NAOKI HIGASHIDA

Adele paced herself slowly along the wiggle road with Luke by her side, his hand resting companionably on the arm of Nadine's chair while Arabelle wuffed and snuffled along, nose to the ground, on the opposite side. About half the year in West Michigan, she mused, from mid-April through early November, the area is awash in color, at certain times a phantasmagoria of visual stimulation. Adele supposed one could say the other five-and-a-half months were washed out. Thankfully, she had never viewed them that way.

Truth was, she appreciated browns and grays. Not that she was a melancholy person. Well, perhaps that adjective did define her personality, but only in a mellowed out sort of way. Adele enjoyed playing with her very amateur digital photos, finding it fun to alter a snapshot to a sepia image, perhaps allowing a touch of red here or there to emerge. She was reminded of that unforgettable scene in the movie *Schindler's List* of the little girl in the red coat wandering unattended through the grayed-out crowds in the emptying ghetto. Sameness, she reflected, invites and accentuates contrast, and contrast allows people to hone in on some of life's most subtle finery. It was easier for her to reflect, as now, *after* a season of sensual bombardment—one of the upsides of late fall and winter.

All of this was particularly true this year. Nadine's around-the-corner demise fed Adele's melancholia. Indeed, her sister's face epitomized in her mind the grayed-out signature of the coming period. After sixty-seven years of intense life, Nadine's eyes were losing the luster that had characterized her outlook, slowly letting go, as though it required inordinate energy to maintain that gleam. Still, the increasingly enfeebled woman revealed in her gaze a resigned comfort—perhaps even a hint of relief—rather than pain or fear.

Nadine's life had been happy in its way. For the most part she had known only love—on that score Adele couldn't fault herself, despite her inevitable periodic frustration and impatience. Her older sister had virtually lunged her way through the years, tilted slightly forward as though in eagerness to embrace the onrushing moment, whatever it might bring. In this particular moment her eyes darted back and forth, taking in detail along her favorite route with a hint of the gusto displayed by Arabelle and Luker.

Luke

"At the height of laughter, the universe is flung into a kaleidoscope of new possibilities." —JEAN HOUSTON

A large pile of windblown leaves—now brown, gray, and even black (they, too, seemed to have relinquished their intensity)—

trapped behind a tree trunk caught Luke's eye. In characteristic fashion the boy surrendered himself to the call, joined by Arabelle in all-out frolic, bounding and leaping and kicking and diving. Far from disinterested, Luker's great-aunt, who no longer spoke, began gesturing furiously, arms extended outward and then circling back repeatedly toward her chest in a motion reminding Adele of a desire to internalize a Valentine heart.

Luke, needing no second invitation, began bombarding his great-aunt with leaves, covering her already swathed head, her lap, her arms and legs. At Nadine's delighted squeals Adele found herself spurred to action. While Arabelle danced circles around the wheelchair, Nadine's sister and great-nephew buried her in nature's brittle bounty, memorializing a life that had on its own level been lived well and fully. Nadine's glee epitomized for her sister that subtle finery of the sepia season.

Jovanny

"Piglet sidled up to Pooh from behind. 'Pooh!' he whispered.
'Yes, Piglet?' 'Nothing,' said Piglet, taking Pooh's paw.
'I just wanted to be sure of you.'" —A. A. MILNE

Jovanny, decked out in his new duds, sat importantly, erect and still despite dangling feet, next to a squirming Rory, whose hand was grasped firmly in Adele's. Mama had never looked so happy—or pretty—and Gage in his new suit was impressive too. The novelty of calling Gage by that new name—*Daddy*—had been introduced just that morning as a special surprise for *after* the service. Jovanny felt as though that magical name were already on his lips, pressing to find its way out.

Soon enough the brief ceremony was over. Jovanny, tired from having already endured a photo session, found himself trotted up, his hand in Adele's with Rory on her opposite side, to Mama and Gage—er, Daddy. Some of those in the line, he noticed, shook their hands, while others planted kisses, especially on Mama. When Jovanny's turn came he met them both with effusive, thigh-height hugs. He worried a little about knocking Mama over but was relieved to see her smiling at him big, with unexplained tears in her eyes. Gage scooped him up, Rory in his other arm, kissing them both on their cheeks and then in their hair.

"Hi, Daddy," Jovanny intoned softly, trying it out. The word sounded good and was, as promised, met with enthusiasm by the person to whom it was addressed. *Jovanny had acquired a daddy!*

Grant

"Step parents are not around to replace a biological parent, rather to augment a child's life experience." —AZRIEL JOHNSON

Almost immediately behind them in the reception line, Grant couldn't help but clasp the other three-year-old's hand a little more tightly. No, he wasn't the jealous type, but it was hard to feel entitled when this other daddy—the *real* one—stood by, for the moment delighting in another's sons. Grant's thoughts, tumbled like sheets in a dryer, didn't at the moment feel very Christian. This doubt would pass and resurface, he knew, perhaps many times.

Commitment to Lauren's children would pose no problem! It was a felt lack of prerogative to that dedication, and more especially to its three precious subjects, that troubled Lauren's fiancé. His ill-formed wish that preoccupation with another's kids might wean Gage's heart from his own—bring about a love amnesia of sorts—was as ludicrous as it was unfair. Life for himself as a daddy would be so much easier, though, without a rival—in this case a *friend rival*, appearing to wait in the wings. For a moment he was almost jealous of Gage with Mallory's kids, who at least had no remotely interested daddies to emphasize the surrogacy aspect of the arrangement.

God wasn't going to make Grant's father/child privilege too easy, but with his help the situation would be doable. At that moment—through God's grace, he knew—Grant's commitment expanded to fully embrace his friend and brother in the Lord. While Lauren's continued custody would never be an issue,

Grant would share Gage's children, each one a sacred trust from the Lord to all the involved adults. He and Lauren, with input from Adele and, in a more limited sense, from Grant and Mallory, would assume and maintain this stewardship role together. No, there would probably never be legal adoptions in Grant's future, no changes of last name for the children. But neither, with the Spirit's empowerment, would he suffer any real anxiety about his right or ability to love and nurture.

Luke took the initiative a moment later when the line reached Gage. Wriggling free of Grant's hand, the little boy threw his right arm around his daddy's leg, turning to hug Grant's, with equal enthusiasm, with the left. Like a tree climber settled in the crook above the trunk, secure between its main, supporting branches, the little one beamed his pleasure.

Rory

*"Dads are most ordinary men turned by love into heroes,
adventurers, story-teller, singers of songs."* —PAM BROWN

"I have a daddy!" Rory announced with gusto to Luke.

"Me too!" Luke put in, as though the coincidence were hilarious. "That's a funny joke!"

"You guys have the same daddy!" Lannie pointed out matter-of-factly. "You're almost like brothers." This was funnier still. Both responded with gleeful laughter. This time it was Lexie who cut in with new information: "And you're gonna have another daddy, Luker!"

"Another daddy!" The boys repeated this in shrill synch, both finding it beyond funny; certainly neither had been so privileged in the past. A ripple of appreciative laughter from the gathered reception guests within the small room floated in the background.

It was Jovanny who put the icing on the cake. "What about God" he suggested, "—the *Father?*" The gathered older children solemnly considered this point, nodding their agreement that this did indeed count.

Adele

"Only you know your circumstances, your energy level, the needs of your children, and the emotional demands of your other obligations. Be wise during intensive seasons of your life."—CHIEKO N. OKAZAKI

As pleased as she was about both weddings, Adele found herself unable to shake a pensive mood when it came to her three youngest grandchildren. Lauren had never been less than a devoted mother, but since the family's move-in before Luke's birth Adele's youngest had handed over much of the responsibility. Was this, Adele wondered now, based on some tacit mutual agreement stemming from her own, hardly hidden, desire to be hands-on with the children? Was there an unintended rivalry Lauren had recognized and to which she had graciously consented? Or had she, finding herself reestablished in her mother's household, fallen back into a semi-dependent role? Adele wasn't sure, nor was she certain it constituted a problem either way. More of a fact, calling now for some circumstantial adjustment.

The nearly concurrent introduction of Grant and reintroduction of Gage into the picture had changed everything—for the better for all concerned. In terms of all of their futures, Adele couldn't have been happier. But life's course corrections come seldom without some pain, or at least, as in this bittersweet November, some chafing. Nadine's imminent passage played its role, of course. It seemed to the now sixty-four year old as though events were conspiring—no, that was a negative perception—*working together* in a new direction. *For good*, she acceded with a half smile, startled that her groping for an alternate word or phrase had yielded a beloved biblical quote. Yes, *all things working together for good*; how could she have missed that?

Despite the frenetic season, Adele found this sepia time of the year, and increasingly of her life as well, suited for reflection. Thoughts that hadn't entered her mind in years were thrusting their way in—introducing and reintroducing themselves seemingly of their own accord—thoughts about her own, *personal* (she briefly savored that notion) well-being and future and, yes, desires and preferences. With these recognitions came another: she was bone-tired physically and drained emotionally (though not spiritually; this strange year had been good in that regard). Adele, not yet old, had aspirations beyond caregiving and childrearing: interests in volunteering, a shucking of some home- and yard-based responsibility, serious reading (she had long wanted to join a book club), traveling, even grand-parenting (as opposed to parenting grandkids) . . . and the list went on.

The older grandchildren were making their transitions into independence—smoothly, all of them—and she had neither regrets about the quality of her past relationships with them nor misgivings about additional letting go. With regard to the little ones—all six, soon to be seven (she had no intention of differentiating)—Nanna looked forward to the good times and the spoiling that constitute the appropriate role of a grandma. Mallory had every interest in the surrogate grand-parenting Adele had to offer, and the children mutually enjoyed one another's company. But Adele wouldn't overdo—maybe two at a time for some special outings or activities . . .

The longer Adele allowed herself to redirect her thought patterns, the less done in she felt. The exhaustion seemed to lift like a fog, elongating the scope of her gaze. And with it went the ambiguity. She'd been short-sighted of necessity, enjoying life— "always blessed," to use her sister's turn of phrase—but unfulfilled and unaware of the lack. A new (healthy and overdue) selfishness began to take hold of her. Adele, to her surprise, found herself eager for the soon-coming season.

Lauren

"Unconditional love is hard to compete with." —ABBI GLINES

It was Lexie's turn to accompany Momma on a holiday tour of Walmart. Despite the showy reminders of the season—lest preoccupied shoppers forget, Lauren thought—her list was practical: a toothbrush for Lannie, children's Motrin, lip gloss, razors, AA batteries, fuel filter injector cleaner, and Gain detergent. Unlike Adele, who price-shopped, generally settling for store brands, Lauren's one indulgence was scent. When in the market for any product for which fragrance might be a purchase variable, it was invariably her determinant. Tonight, wending her way through the shampoos (which she didn't need but enjoyed), unscrewing lids and sharing whiffs with Lexie, Lauren was in her element. Easy to please, Adele always conceded, but frustrating to accompany through a store.

Navigating the cart past the grocery section toward automotive, the pair was startled by an unexpected tinkling that, while vaguely Christmassy, still seemed incongruent. A vague commotion in the wine aisle suggested that other shoppers thought the same, and mother and daughter peered in that direction. A third of the way down the aisle, on the top shelf, a jiggling, giggling automated baby doll with an obnoxious laugh had been left atop some of the wares; the motion was having something of a domino effect, with wine bottles up and down the line vibrating and clinking merrily.

The scene was amusing to most, but Lexie's alarmed response was urgent: "Her needs me!" The distraught child becoming more insistent as Lauren continued past the aisle, she turned the cart and returned. Sheepish, Lauren snatched up the abandoned waif and placed it in the waiting arms of its adoptive mother.

Adele's Devotion: A November Reading

READY?

"'Believe in the light while you have the light, so that you may become children of light.'" (JOHN 12:36)

Jesus was preparing his disciples for his coming death. In the next verse John goes on to comment that Jesus left and hid himself from his disciples. Was he in some small way preparing them for his leave-taking?

I chuckle at George Carlin's "Weather forecast for tonight: dark." That's only provisionally true, of course (Jesus has risen and ascended, and the Spirit disseminates light in and through us). But how ready are we for the full radiance to come? Frederick Buechner addressed this issue movingly: "People are prepared for everything except for the fact that beyond the darkness of their blindness there is a great light. They are prepared for a mustard-seed kingdom of God no bigger than the eye of a newt but not for the great banyan it becomes with birds in its branches singing Mozart. They are prepared for the potluck supper at First Presbyterian but not for the marriage supper of the lamb." To what degree are you anticipating Christ's light?

December

Lauren

"When I stopped seeing my mother with the eyes of a child, I saw the woman who helped me give birth to myself." —NANCY FRIDAY

"Hey, Mom!" Lauren caught Adele, seated over coffee at the kitchen table, with a backhanded hug around the neck and shoulders.

"Hey back! What's up?"

"Now *why* would something need to be up?"

"You're right. Let's try that again. How's it going?"

"I think you know the answer! Seriously, I just want to thank you for everything you've done. I know words aren't enough, but they're what I have to offer."

"And more than sufficient. Don't ever think the benefit has been one-directional."

"I know—and I don't. . . . You *are* still gonna have my back for babysitting, right?"

"There it is, that agenda! You know I'm kidding. We'll see how that one goes once you get settled. Definitely not a fulltime commitment."

"I was kidding too. I wouldn't expect that either. . . . Mom, you know I love you, right?"

"Never a doubt. And back atcha!" Setting down the steaming mug, Adele turned around to enfold her youngest in an embrace.

Jovanny

*"I was made to feel I could do things. If you get
this feeling early and can hold it until you're 15,
you tend to never lose it."* —JOHN UPDIKE

Jovanny's smile was irrepressible. Not only had Mr. Cruz awarded him a first-place certificate for a running race, but he'd been hand-picked by Mr. Dekker, the music teacher, for a solo singing part in the upcoming Christmas program, to take place on the Thursday evening of the last week of school prior to vacation. And all of this after being awarded a role as one of the three wise men in the Sunday school program, for which the children were practicing songs each week. (Daisy was equally excited about her angel choir part in that performance.)

Even at his tender age the boy was able to make a comparison between the situation this year and last. And that comparison, thanks to input from both his Sunday school teacher and his new daddy, was set against the backdrop of the biggest surprise ever—a God who loved him and his family, news he could neither have guessed nor anticipated!

Gage

*"It is a sweet thing that we serve a dissatisfied God
who has destinations in mind for us that we would never
choose for ourselves. It really is a good thing that he will
not be satisfied until he has gotten us exactly where he
created us and re-created us to be."* —PAUL DAVID TRIPP

The wedding was behind, the home situation settled, the training aspect of the new job gradually giving way to independent work. Gage was slowly, and proudly, accumulating his own tools, though the boss's were available to him in the interim. Mallory's pregnancy was following a carefully monitored course, the obstetrician aware of her undiagnosed preeclampsia the last time around.

The older children, first graders in different classes, were thriving in school. Jovanny, fine-boned and now in particular rail thin, was experiencing a growth spurt; he exceeded the petite Daisy by inches in height and liked to play the big brother . . . to her big sister. Both roles served a purpose, and they didn't appear to be mutually exclusive. School attendance was no longer a problem; there were no more "down" days due to Gage's drunken state or Mallory's condition. Keeping Daisy and Jovanny in the same district via exercising the "school of choice" option was working. Gage was able in the mornings to drop them off and still make it to work on time. And an after-school program—during which homework, with guidance, was accomplished—met the need until he could pick them up.

The move had relieved little Rory of much of the boredom that had characterized school days last year. The opportunity to play and explore without competition seemed to meet a need for him. More importantly, the family was settling in to faith and fellowship, new realities that still awed Mallory, for whom friends remained a novelty never before visualized or even considered. Given her dysfunctional girlhood, keeping "outsiders" at bay had been a felt need affecting even her early school interactions.

As far as the other three children (his and Lauren's) were concerned, Gage was willing to yield to his friend Grant in his desire to function as daddy. It had become evident that Adele considered both families her own, and get-togethers would be inclusive and comfortable.

What a difference a year could make! But only with, and in, God! *That* reality still tended to floor Gage, who only months earlier would never have dreamed the transition possible.

Lannie

"Baking cookies is comforting, and cookies are the sweetest little bit of comfort food. They are very bite-sized and personal." —SANDRA LEE

The watched plate of just-baked Christmas cookies waited provocatively on the table. Lannie had parked herself in the chair, elbows on the placemat and head in hands, waiting for the hot cocoa water to boil. As Adele stepped out of the kitchen to turn down the TV volume for Nadine, the seven year old inched her hand toward the plate. Her announcement, evidently intended for no one in particular, was matter-of-fact and barely audible: "Nanna, I'm just gonna check this cookie to see if it's okay or not okay." An unseen thumbs up. A moment later, as Adele stepped back into the room: "Yours is okay too."

Mallory

"The arms of love encompass you with your present, your past, your future, the arms of love gather you together." —ANTOINE DE SAINT-EXUPÉRY

Gage, Mallory, and their three were joining the extended family for an early December pre-Christmas dinner celebration (consisting of pizza, breadsticks, pop, and ice cream contributed by Grant and Lauren) at Adele's home. Nadine's rapidly deteriorating health, along with at times overlapping brief visits from all four of Adele's older children and their families, was making for a hectic Advent with little opportunity for Adele to leave the house. What holiday decorating had been done was also thanks to Grant and Lauren and their enthusiastic trio. Picture-perfect preparation was furthest from anyone's mind, allowing the children opportunity to spread their emergent creative wings. The tree was lit, carols played, and the contagious happiness of the little ones pervaded the scene.

The evening's festivities were to include modest gifts for the six children, from Mallory's side all carefully chosen from the plenty with which the family had been gifted months earlier. Lannie had taken Daisy under her wing (despite the difference of one year in school, the two were close in age). As the oldest on both sides, they shared some common big-sister traits, though Lannie was much more effusive, not to mention generous to a fault. Daisy, who had less experience with friendship, let alone being feted in so exclusive a way, maintained a star-struck aura, not knowing quite what to do with the onrush of new experiences.

Lexie and Jovanny, both sensitive and quiet by nature, amused themselves at the kitchen table decorating construction paper gingerbread people with paste, cotton balls, google eyes, ribbon, buttons, stars, fabric scraps, and other decorative paraphernalia also provided by Lauren. But the duo of three year olds, Luke and Rory, gave vent to their joint enthusiasm without reserve. The two meshed with a totality that touched the watching adults. Gage in particular, given his unique investment in all six children, was flushed with pride, while Grant and Lauren observed the little ones with appreciation.

In the end, though, it was to be Mallory who stole the show with an announcement of her pregnancy, already well along—and known for some time by Lauren and Adele, along with, of course, Gage. This left Grant the only adult to register unfeigned surprise, though even Nadine managed a smile. No one questioned that four children would be a handful, but given the circumstances of the previous year the well wishes were genuine. Mallory had started early with prenatal care at the clinic, and a recent ultrasound had brought the welcome news of another little girl. Grant, the articulate pastor's son, led the group in an impromptu prayer, asking for blessing and offering thanks. The two older girls, who understood the significance, were beside themselves with glee, and Jovanny beamed silently in the background, his eyes fixed on Mama's face.

Rory

"One of the things that Christmas reminds us is that Jesus Christ was once a child."—HARK HERALD SARMIENTO

"Why is Christmas?"

"Why is Christmas what?"

"Why is Christmas *Christmas*?"

"Like why do we have Christmas?"

"Uh-huh."

"You had a birthday, right?"

"Uh-huh."

"The day you were born, when you were just new, that was your very first birthday, right?"

"Uh-huh."

"And every year you have another one. It's to celebrate *you!*"

"Yeah! *Me.*"

"Christmas is like that too. It's the day we celebrate when Jesus was tiny and new. He's all grown up now, and he lives in heaven. But he still has birthdays. He loves you, Rory!"

"Me too!"

"You love Jesus too?"

"Uh huh. And you, Nanna."

"And I love you. And Luke too. Come on, guys. Let's have a hugger!"

Grant

"However many blessings we expect from God, His infinite liberality will always exceed all our wishes and our thoughts." —JOHN CALVIN

Grant and Lauren were sharing the couch, she sideways against his arm, wriggling her stocking-clad toes in the snuggly throw slung across its opposite arm. The lighted tree twinkled in the window, leaving soft plops of colored reflection on the drifted front yard visible through the picture window. Night had fallen early, but the white glow from the accumulated ground cover belied the hour. A drowsing Aunt Nadine added her unique brand of tranquility to the scene; the nearly continuous carols playing softly in the background were primarily for her sake. Mom, her oldest son, Jarrod, and his wife, Leone, sat at the kitchen table savoring after-dinner conversation, and the three children were enjoying the attention of their teenaged cousins in the den.

The couple had spent much of the day house hunting with a realtor—not for an apartment but for a real house, a three-bedroom with a den and a fenced-in backyard and a basement play area to accommodate a growing family. Sticker shock had hit hard, even though Grant in his responsible way had over several years saved the amount of a respectable down payment.

Lauren, undaunted, glowed with anticipation, though Grant, who had hoped for more square footage, not to mention a decade or two newer in a slightly more appealing neighborhood, was pensive. It hadn't taken long in the relationship for him to recognize that it took very little to please his bride-to-be. And he had no doubt she would make short work of making a home of any house they might purchase. But saddling themselves with a house of any kind was no small undertaking. The kind of upward mobility attained in part by "flipping" houses every few years had never appealed to him. And improvement in the economy had fueled a pent-up demand that was inciting the realtor to encourage a quick decision—a decision Grant didn't feel ready to make, not, at least, based on the caliber of homes they'd been seeing all day.

He'd done his share of relocating throughout his childhood. What he and Lauren really wanted was a place to call their own, a center from which to put down roots; branch out; and grow *within*, not away from. Grant had no problem with home improvement projects—especially in light of the prospect of working with *this* partner!—but neither did he relish the idea of a fixer-upper. He envisioned an instant home for his wife and kids—*his* kids; he liked the sound of that! Gradual, modest improvements would be icing on the cake, celebrated one lick at a time.

At that moment Adele and Jarrod wandered into the room, each with two mugs in hand—from which wafted the scent of hot cider—one of which each handed off to a couch inhabitant. Lauren's brother Jarrod, settled in Nadine's rocker, lost no time in opening an evidently preplanned conversation. He asked first how the house hunting had gone, to which Grant replied truthfully. At that point Jarrod leaned forward: "What about a house on par with this one?"

"Well, yeah! Of course! It has everything we want. But so far what we're seeing is falling a little short. Do you know of one?"

"As a matter of fact I—we, that is, do—yes. What would you think of this one?"

"*This one!?* Oh, my gorgeous!" shrieked Lauren (she'd picked up the exclamation from Lannie), sitting bolt upright, managing a neat save of the momentarily slanting mug. Her childhood home held so many cherished memories, for herself and her children, not to mention featuring every nonnegotiable on her own and Grant's short list.

"For real! I never dreamed . . . " The articulate Grant was uncharacteristically dumbfounded, causing Adele and Lauren to break into laughter suggesting far more than mutual amusement.

"Mom isn't going to need this big place for one person, and upkeep and yard work are getting to be a bit much. She and Leone and I have done a little looking ourselves, and Mom's fallen in love with a condo on a lake just a couple of miles from here. It's got a guestroom but not quite enough space for a boomerang family" (that with a smile in his little sister's direction). "Your down payment would get her in, and from there you can start making monthly payments to Mom. All four of us"—meaning Lauren's siblings—"got our heads together a while ago already. Mom has a fairly good idea about our inheritance, and we've all agreed to Lauren's getting her share—the bulk of it, at least—a little early."

"Hopefully more than a little," Adele put in. "At this point I'm not anticipating an early departure." Her eyes strayed to her sister in the bed, but without sorrow. Nadine's leave-taking would in many ways be a blessing—for Nadine herself but also for Adele in light of other possible scenarios she could envision.

"I'm speechless!" Grant put in.

"To state the obvious!" his fiancée teased, jabbing him in the ribs with her elbow.

"No need to wait. We can make the arrangements effective any time. Mom would like to put in a bid on that condo, and she and Aunt Nadine don't mind sharing *your* place for the time being!"

Lauren and Grant rose to their feet as one and ran, Lauren to her big brother and Grant to his mother-in-law-to-be, enfolding them in hugs that brought tears to both women. The five kids and Leone, sensing the commotion, gathered in the archway between the living room and the kitchen, all grinning.

"Merry Christmas!" shouted Leon, the children's oldest cousin, to which all responded with whoops and cheers. Quietly turning off the background music, Adele launched into a carol, all of the others, with the exceptions of the oldest and youngest, joining in. Nadine, awake, greeted the scene with a barely detectable smile, her gaze upturned and far away.

Luke

"Would Christ have made a child the standard of faith if He had known that it was not capable of understanding His words?" —D. L. MOODY

Two or three times now Adele had been caught inadvertently interrupting Luke's devotions. Just this morning on a pre-Christmas errand (Lauren was home with Nadine and the girls), Nanna and her grandson had mutually enjoyed a children's CD of gospel choruses, a favorite Adele played regularly for Luke's backseat benefit. She couldn't get enough of his off-key voice enthusiastically chiming in on some of the lyrics.

Adele found it natural to join in, an impulse Luke politely checked: "Please be quiet, Nanna. I'm singing to Jesus."

Daisy

"Advent creates people, new people." —DIETRICH BONHOEFFER

The baby theme, so intrinsic to Christmas, had an intense impact on Daisy. The fact that Jesus had come to Earth in the way he did—as a *homeless* baby—affected her deeply. Why, even the inn, the *hotel*, wouldn't rent a room to Mary and Joseph, and their baby was coming, just as Mama's had come in the big house in North Carolina. Daisy remembered those nights at the rest stop, huddled in the station wagon trying to keep warm. Was it like that when Mary's baby came in the shed (she wasn't sure of the appropriate analogy, though she was pretty certain the cows and sheep and pigs could get him—could lick him with their scratchy tongues and touch him rough or maybe make him dirty).

The thing was, though: Jesus *understood!* He *got* her . . . Daisy! Everything about her made sense to him! Daisy had no reason to be ashamed before Jesus. He had started out *just like her.* But he had become a King, a strong, loving King who had a special spot in his heart for her, and Jovanny, and Rory! The shame was beginning to dissipate; she could feel it. For Mama and for her too. And a new baby was coming—a girl! She'd heard Mama say that, and she just loved baby girls. Like Mrs. Jillian's. Daisy would be the *best* big sister! She already tried with Jovanny and Rory, but this would be different . . . Daisy visualized a new beginning, not just for her little sister but for herself as well.

Nadine

"When leaves die do they go to heaven?" —ERIC SUTTON

There was nothing dramatic about the end—inhalation, exhalation . . . *wait for it!* . . . no: a suspension, a letting go. Sixty-seven years of God's faithfulness, sixty-seven years of reliable breathing—in again, out again—and then . . . no more. Nadine the reliable, the blissfully unaware, Nadine the undemanding, the gleeful, lover of pranks and games and Jesus, was no more . . . because God took her. Without fanfare on Christmas evening the Father determined the moment was right to bear her back to himself. *Well done, good and faithful servant! Enter your rest! What a surprise when you awaken!*

Adele, Lauren, and Grant were the sole witnesses. It seemed as though Aunt Nadine had held off in deference to the children. No, surely that nuance of timing was God's. At any rate, the moment of demise was serene—a slipping, and a fall, a plop as light as the purest snowflake. Nadine was home!

At Adele's request, Grant reached for the Bible and read softly from Ecclesiastes 3, emphasizing verses 1–2: "There is a time for everything, and a season for every activity under the heavens: a time to be born and a time to die." Ad-libbing, he reflected that, as each year circles back to its beginning and surges into a new one, time begins to overwrap itself. As the years continue to make their circuit, joy overlays sorrow and vice versa. Human experience ebbs and flows, waxes and wanes, and the circle gradually picks up new generational players and drops others. "Think back," he invited his future wife and mother-in-law, "on your own lifetime of joys and sorrows, ups and downs—all the contrasts from Ecclesiastes 3. How has God remained constant through it all?"

Lexie

"It is difficult to realize how great a part of all that is cheerful and delightful in the recollections of our own life is associated with trees." —WILSON FLAGG

Two evenings later, it was Lexie's turn with Adele; the two, walking Arabelle, were admiring the bolded white outlines showcasing the skeletal bone structures of snow-encased trees on the park side of the wiggle road. But Lexie's gaze turned to encompass the scene from the other side: "Nanna, I like the snow best on the everlasting trees."

Evergreen! recognized Adele immediately. She paused momentarily to savor that word—lovely and hopeful in itself.

Adele

"When you look at your life the greatest happinesses are family happinesses." —DR. JOYCE BROTHERS

While Arabelle snuffled in the snow, evidently having caught a whiff of something unseen below, Adele surveyed the transformed horizon with its gently rolling, glassy sheet of white. There was something pristine and exquisite about an untouched field of deep, new-fallen snow, she acknowledged as her eyes panned the undisturbed blanket over the park from her vantage point on the wiggle road—a picture of newness, the suggestion of a fresh, unsoiled start. The storm, a gentle but extended one, had coincided this year with Christmas Day, and a new year—another January through December with all its serendipities and sadness and sunshine—beckoned just beyond that horizon. Tucked in its shared comforter, everything looked crisp and united by winter's great white leveler. The weed-choked yards, she mused, flowed seamlessly into the manicured plots next door. And the sun on the snow, or the moon on the snow, afforded the darker world of winter a welcome, uniform 24/7 glow. No, all might not be right with the world, or at least not everywhere, but it was well with her soul. And right now that counted for a lot.

Adele's Devotion: A December Reading

SPIRAL

"It is God's will that you should be sanctified."
(1 THESSALONIANS 4:3)

"Year's end," reflects Hal Borland, "is neither an end nor a beginning, but a going on, with all the wisdom that experience can instill in us." Borland's picture isn't one of a continuous circle but of a winding spiral, inching its way upward with every revolution.

While I don't believe that unregenerate human nature progresses, I recognize that individuals grow in experience. More importantly, the Spirit-inspired process of sanctification causes the Christian to make continuous strides in the direction of godliness. Take a moment to assess your journey over the now waning year. Can you detect an upward trajectory? Are you closer to God now than at its beginning? More mellow, patient, or trusting? More regular in prayer? Pause to thank the Spirit for the gift of sanctification. Your progression, after all, is 100 percent a gift.

www.ingramcontent.com/pod-product-compliance
Lightning Source LLC
Chambersburg PA
CBHW061135200626
46817CB00016B/1633